Sweet
Dreams

Sweet Dreams

ROBIN JONES GUNN

BETHANY HOUSE PUBLISHERS
MINNEAPOLIS, MINNESOTA 55438

Sweet Dreams
Revised edition 1999
Copyright © 1994, 1999
Robin Jones Gunn

Edited by Janet Kobobel Grant
Cover illustration and design by Lookout Design Group, Inc.

This story is a work of fiction. All characters and events are the product of the author's imagination. Any resemblance to any person, living or dead, is coincidental. Text has been revised and updated by the author.

Focus on the Family books are available at special quantity discounts when purchased in bulk by corporations, organizations, churches, or groups. Special imprints, messages, and excerpts can be produced to meet your needs. For more information, contact: Resource Sales Group, Focus on the Family, 8605 Explorer Drive, Colorado Springs, CO 80920; or phone (800) 932-9123.

A Focus on the Family book published by
Bethany House Publishers
A Ministry of Bethany Fellowship International
11400 Hampshire Avenue South
Bloomington, Minnesota 55438
www.bethanyhouse.com

Printed in the United States of America by
Bethany Press International, Bloomington, Minnesota 55438

Library of Congress Cataloging-in-Publication Data

Gunn, Robin Jones, 1955–
    Sweet dreams / by Robin Jones Gunn.
        p.   cm. — (The Christy Miller Series ; 11)
    Summary: Christy Miller learns to be a friend by letting go of both her best friend, Katie, and her boyfriend, Todd, when he takes a short-term mission assignment.
    ISBN 1-56179-732-4
    [1. Friendship—Fiction. 2. Christian life—Fiction.] I. Title.
II. Series: Gunn, Robin Jones, 1955–   Christy Miller Series ; 11.
PZ7.G972Sw   1994
[Fic]—dc20   94-6239
                                                                    CIP
                                                                    AC

02 03 04 05 06 07 08 09 / 16 15 14 13 12 11 10 9 8 7 6

For my brother,

Dr. Kevin Travis Jones

Contents

CHAPTER ONE

What Else Could Go Wrong?

"We need to have the team captains in the very front," Christy Miller called out to the girls lined up for the yearbook picture of the Kelley High volleyball team.

Flipping her nutmeg brown hair over her shoulder and closing one eye, Christy sized up the group in her camera's viewfinder. This would be her last photo for the yearbook, and she was eager to finish.

"Where's Katie?" she asked. "And who's the other captain?"

"I am," said a tall girl kneeling in the front.

"Squeeze in on the right, you guys," Christy directed. "There, that's good. Does anyone know where Katie is?"

"She's not in the locker room," one girl said. "I was just there."

"She's probably off with Michael," a girl in the middle row observed.

"Yeah, well," said another girl, "if I was going to fall in love, that's who I'd want to do it with, too."

"Did you see them today?" a girl with sandy blonde hair asked. "They had on matching 'Save the Rain Forest' T-shirts. And yesterday Katie said Michael was applying to go on a trip to the Amazon this summer with some environmental group. I bet she goes with him.''

Christy's heart began to pound faster. This was her best friend they were talking about. Katie wouldn't run off to the jungle without telling Christy about it. At least, six months ago she wouldn't have. But ever since Michael had entered Katie's life, Christy and Katie had grown farther and farther apart. It felt like a stab wound to hear these girls display more knowledge of Katie's life than Christy had.

"Just take the shot," one of the girls said. "We have to get back to class."

"Okay," Christy said, focusing the camera. "Can you squeeze a little closer in the back row? Great. Perfect. Okay, you guys, smile!" She snapped the picture, and the girls immediately dispersed.

Hurrying back to her class, Christy thought, *This silence thing has gone on long enough. I'm going to talk to Katie today and do whatever it takes to get our friendship back on track.*

In a few months they would be graduating from high school. They had had so many great times together. It couldn't end with this icy standoff between them.

Everything had changed the day Katie met Michael, and Christy had done little to hold on to their friendship. Of course, Christy had been busy with her own boyfriend, Todd. That was a relationship she had waited a long time for. Now, nearly every weekend she and Todd were together, and she hadn't felt the need to work things out with Katie until the girls on the volleyball team displayed their superior knowledge of the events in Katie's life.

Right after school, Christy began to carry out her plan. She knew where Katie parked her car in the school lot, so Christy decided to wait by Katie's car. When she showed up, Christy would say, "I've been a horrible friend for not being supportive of your relationship with Michael. I've missed your friendship, and I want us to find a way to be close again." *That's* what she would say.

Christy found Katie's car and waited nearly twenty minutes. There was no sign of Katie anywhere. Dozens of cars zoomed past her, leaving the parking lot looking like an emptied pizza box with the few remaining cars scattered around like leftover chunks of pizza toppings. She was about ready to give up and leave when she heard Michael's slightly beat-up sports car roar into the parking lot.

I'll say, 'Hi, Michael,' and I'll smile at him and be nice, Christy told herself. But she barely had a chance to look at him.

The passenger door of his car opened before Michael had even come to a complete stop. Katie lurched out, slamming the door. Michael popped the car into gear and bolted past them, leaving a puff of exhaust to envelop Christy and Katie's first face-to-face encounter in more than two months.

"Hi," Christy said shyly. "How are you doing?"

Katie stared at Christy, her eyes swollen and red. "Why are you here?"

"Well, I, um . . . you missed the yearbook picture with your volleyball team."

"You waited here to tell me that?"

"No, actually, I waited here because I wanted to talk to you."

"I don't believe this," Katie said, shaking her head so that her short, straight, copper-colored hair swished like silk tassels.

"Believe what?" Christy asked, shrinking back. Katie had no problem speaking her mind, and it looked as though she was in the mood to let someone have it. Christy didn't want it to be her.

"I can't believe this," Katie said again, groping in her backpack for her car keys. "I don't think I can talk to you right now. This is too weird."

"What's too weird?"

Katie stood still, her green eyes narrowing into slits, scrutinizing Christy's expression. "This is just too much of a God thing for me right now. I have to go." Then, jerking her car door open, she climbed in and started up the engine.

Christy didn't know if she should knock on the window and try to get Katie to pay attention to her or if she should run across the parking lot, jump in her own car, and chase Katie. Before Christy had time to decide, Katie jammed her car into drive and squealed out of the school parking lot.

" 'Too much of a God thing'—what's that supposed to mean?" Christy muttered as she picked up her belongings and lugged them across the lot to her lonely-looking car. "Do I have bad timing, or what? She and Michael obviously had a fight. Maybe after she's had some time to cool down, I'll try talking with her. Why did I wait by her car anyway? I should have called her. It's easier to talk on the phone."

"Christy!" came a familiar voice across the lot. It was Fred, one of the other yearbook photographers. Fred was okay in a let's-just-be-friends kind of way. Still, something about him bugged her.

"I'm glad you're still here," he said. "Did you take the picture of the volleyball team?"

"Yes, and I know it's due tomorrow."

"Why don't you and I drop it off at the one-hour photo place together? I'll treat you to a Coke while we're waiting."

"No thanks," Christy said, unlocking her door and getting inside.

"Okay, then an ice cream," Fred amiably suggested.

"I really need to get home, Fred. I have a ton of homework. I'll drop it off on my way home and pick it up tomorrow."

"You're planning on staying after school tomorrow to finish the layout, aren't you?"

"Yes, I'll be here."

"I did it!" Fred said, his face full of glee. "I finally got you to say yes to something I asked. We're on a roll, Christy. It can only get better from here. So do you want to go to the prom with me?"

"No!" Christy said. This was only the fifteenth time he had asked her.

Fred looked undaunted. "Not a problem. You still have six weeks to change your mind."

"I'll see you tomorrow, Fred," Christy said.

"I'll be looking forward to it," he responded cheerfully. He waved and smiled so that his crooked front tooth stuck out. Jogging to his car parked on the other side of the lot, he drove off on his merry way.

Christy stuck her key in the ignition to start her car. Nothing happened. She jiggled the key and tried again. Nothing.

I don't believe this! What else could go wrong? Christy thought, climbing out of the car and slamming the door. With deliberate steps she marched back to the school building to call her dad.

About fifteen minutes later, he pulled up in his white truck. He still had on his overalls from the Hollandale Dairy. He was a large man with reddish hair and bushy red eyebrows. It was embarrassing to have to call her dad to come start her car. She was glad no one was around to see the rescue.

"Did you leave your lights on?" Dad asked when he hopped out of the truck with jumper cables in hand.

"I don't think so."

"Go ahead and pop the hood. We'll try giving the battery some juice."

Christy's dad connected the two car batteries, letting his truck run for a few minutes before saying, "Get in and start her up."

Christy turned the key, and the engine immediately turned over. She smiled her relieved thanks to her dad. Embarrassing or not, it was nice to have a dad who came to the rescue.

"I'll follow you home," Dad said after he had disconnected the cables and slammed down her hood.

They reached home with no problems. Christy thanked her dad and then went straight to her room and flopped on her bed. At nearly the same instant, the phone rang.

"Christy," Mom called from down the hallway, "telephone."

Christy forced her long legs down the hallway and picked up the phone. She heard Todd's familiar "Hey, how's it going?"

"Don't ask," she said.

"Bad day?"

"It didn't start out that way, but the last hour or so has been pretty frustrating." Christy ran through the details, deleting the part about Fred asking her to the prom. "The worst part is," she said, "I feel as if I don't know how to make things right with Katie. Everything I try blows up in my face. I guess I should call her or go over to her house. I hate things being unsettled like this."

"Good idea. Let me know how it goes."

"That's all the advice you have for me? Aren't you going to tell me what to say?"

"No."

"Todd, it's not going to be that easy."

"Sure, it will."

"She'll probably yell at me."

"So she yells at you. At least it'll get you two communicating."

"But then what do I say? Do I go over the stuff I've told her before about how she shouldn't be dating Michael because he's not a Christian? She won't listen to me. I've tried before to get closer to her and help her see that what she's doing is wrong, but she only pushes me away."

"Then let go," Todd said.

"Let go?"

"Listen, Christy," Todd began. His direct yet gentle tone made her relax a little. "I think sometimes the test of true love for a friend is found not in holding onto that person tighter but in letting them go. Sometimes when we step back and let go, it gives God room to do what He's been trying to do all along. It's like He's been waiting for us to get out of the way."

"So you think I've been in God's way?" Christy asked, feeling a little defensive.

Todd paused before saying, "I think you need to let go. Then you'll know for sure that you're not in the way."

Christy let out a sigh. "Okay, I'll call her and tell her . . . I don't know what I'll tell her. But I'll call her. Pray for me, okay?"

"I always do," Todd said. Then with his familiar "Later," he hung up.

Christy closed her eyes and pictured Todd, her tall, broad-shouldered boyfriend. She could see his screaming silver-blue eyes crinkle at the corners and his chin automatically tilt up like it always did whenever he said "Later." She knew she was lucky to have him. Perhaps "blessed" was a better word.

Christy quickly dialed Katie's number before she had time to think about it. Katie answered on the second ring.

"Hi, it's me. Do you have a minute?"

Dead air filled the space between them.

"Why?" Katie finally said.

Christy wished she had taken the time to plan her words before calling. She spouted off the first thing that came to her mind. "Katie, I want you to know that I'm not going to try to tell you what to do anymore. I know I've been critical of Michael, and I'm sorry. Will you forgive me, Katie?"

Christy hadn't expected to cry, but she did. The tears dripped off her cheeks. She stared at the water droplets on her jeans and waited for Katie to respond.

"I can't talk to you right now," Katie said solemnly.

Christy wanted to argue and somehow convince Katie they needed to talk *now*. That's what would make Christy feel better. Apparently, that wasn't what Katie needed. Did letting go mean not pushing Katie to talk things through?

"Okay," Christy said. "That's fine. Could we maybe talk another time?"

"I promise we'll talk later. I'm just not ready yet."

"All right."

"Okay," Katie said. It sounded as if she was crying, too. Then right before she hung up, she said, "Thanks, Chris."

Christy sat with her back against the hallway wall for a long while after hanging up the phone. This was all so complicated. Everyone had told her that her senior year would be her best year of high school. And true, there had been lots of wonderful things, like being with Todd, working on the school yearbook, and having her job at the pet store.

Yet this unresolved conflict over Michael had taken a chomp out of Christy's heart. She had lost her best friend to a dark-haired exchange student from Ireland who, for the last six months, had occupied Katie's every spare moment. Christy brushed her hair back and wiped her blue-green eyes with the palm of her hand. She felt as though she had lost her best friend. And maybe she had.

CHAPTER TWO

The Organic Tomato

The next morning Christy spotted Michael at his locker. Sucking in a deep breath, she approached him with a smile. If she couldn't make peace directly with Katie, maybe somehow she could open up the communication lines through Michael.

"Hi, Michael," she said.

"Morning," Michael returned. His Irish accent made him sound naturally cheerful, but his face told Christy the opposite. He looked as if he had just gotten up, with his dark hair twisted in uncombed curls at the nape of his neck. He was wearing his favorite baggy shorts, leather sandals, and his overly familiar 'Save the Whales' T-shirt.

"Have you seen Katie yet today?"

"No." His answer was curt.

Christy hesitated and then said, "I don't know if it's even my place to ask, but are you guys okay?"

"What did Katie tell you?"

"Nothing. That's the thing. I haven't talked to her, and I know she was upset yesterday after school. I just wanted to see if everything was okay."

"Look," Michael said, cocking his head and sounding mellow

but looking stern, "you haven't the right."

"The right?" Christy ventured.

"Let's be straight. I know you haven't been favorable toward me since Katie and I started to date. Now that Katie somehow believes your prayers have worked against her, you haven't the right to step in like a vulture, waiting to pick at my bones."

Christy was shocked. "What?" she stammered, but it was too late. Michael had already turned and was maneuvering his way through the congestion in the hallways.

I haven't the right? What do you mean I haven't the right? I'm Katie's best friend!

The bell rang loudly right above Christy's head. She felt like yelling back at it.

Why would Michael say such a thing to me? Why would he say I'm like a vulture? And what does he mean my prayers have worked against her? What's going on here?

Hurrying to her locker, she threw her books inside and wished somehow she could curl up inside, too. She wished it even more when she heard someone call out, "Miss Chris." She knew it had to be Fred.

"Hey, what's with Katie? She was all over my case this morning because she heard we took the volleyball team photo without her."

"What did you tell her?"

"I told her you took it. Wasn't my fault she didn't manage to show up."

"Oh, that's just great. Thanks a lot, Fred. Now she'll never speak to me again!" Christy slammed her locker door and marched down the hall to her first class.

"Sure, she will," Fred said, briskly trotting beside her. "I told her if she wanted to reschedule another photo to talk to you, and you would contact the rest of the team."

"And how am I supposed to do that?" Christy blurted out. "The pictures are due today." Christy suddenly remembered the roll of film was still in her purse.

"Oh, didn't you hear? We have two extra weeks. Miss Wallace found out we're four pages short, so she asked if you and I would work on photo collages. I told her we would work together day and night until we got it just right."

"Why did you tell her that, Fred?"

Fred looked as if he were venturing a wild guess. "Because I'm such a cool guy, and you're dying to spend quality time with me?"

"Guess again, Fred!" Christy spewed and ducked into her classroom just as the final bell rang. She dropped into her chair, feeling horrible. She never should have talked to Fred like that. She wouldn't want anyone treating her that way. And Michael had, that morning. Maybe that's why she turned on Fred.

I'll apologize to him just before yearbook class, Christy decided, trying to focus on the handout the teacher had placed in front of her.

It was a quiz. She had forgotten all about it and hadn't studied at all. This day was not shaping up any better than yesterday.

It didn't get much better until that afternoon. She found Fred in their yearbook class, bending over a table covered with candid photos.

"Fred," Christy said, walking up beside him and gently touching his arm, "I want to apologize for what I said this morning. It was rude, and I'm sorry. I'm kind of under a lot of stress, but that's no excuse."

"It's okay," Fred said without looking up.

There was a pause, and then Christy said, "Should we start working on those collage pages?"

"Sure. I started to look for a few larger ones to sort of get us going, and then I thought we could fill in with some smaller shots."

Miss Wallace walked up and held out a picture of a toddler wearing cowboy boots, a hat, a holster, and a diaper. "Can you guess who this is?"

Fred and Christy looked at the photo and both shook their heads.

"Hal Janssen," Miss Wallace announced.

"You're kidding! Has anyone on the football team seen this?" Christy asked.

"No, Hal's mom brought it in this morning. Won't it look great next to his Cougar of the Week shot when he scored the most points against Vista High?"

"This is perfect!" Fred said, holding up the picture. All his gloom had evaporated. "Now all we need are pictures of Aaron Johnson and Adrian Medina, and our baby hall of fame will be complete."

"This was really a good idea, Fred, collecting all these baby pictures of this year's outstanding students," Miss Wallace said.

"It wasn't my idea," Fred replied quickly. "It was Christy's. I just agreed with her."

Miss Wallace smiled at Christy. "You've done a terrific job, Christy. I think you're a natural at this sort of thing."

Christy could feel a rush of pink to her cheeks. It felt good to know she had finally done something right.

For the next week and a half, Christy kept busy with the yearbook, homework, and her job at the pet store. Over the weekend Todd came up from San Diego, where he was attending college. They went miniature golfing with her eleven-year-old brother and then sat close together on the couch that night, eating popcorn and watching an old black and white movie with Christy's parents. Everything was great. Wonderful. Everything except that she was still waiting for Katie to contact her.

Christy saw Katie and Michael one time at school. They were holding hands, and everything between them seemed perfect. Why, then, wouldn't Katie call Christy or come over and tell her all was well? What had gone on between Katie and Michael that had caused the tension in the parking lot?

When Christy walked into the yearbook class on Thursday, Miss Wallace said, "Christy, I've arranged for you to take another picture of the volleyball team in about ten minutes. They said some of their team members didn't make it for the last shot. Fred offered to take it if you didn't want to, but I thought you would since you've been working on this one all along."

Christy looked over at Fred, who stood a few feet away. He shrugged and said, "Whatever. I didn't know if you were okay with Katie yet."

Christy didn't know either. What would be best for Katie? Would she smile for the picture if Christy was the one behind the camera? Would it be easier if Fred took it?

"Do you mind, Fred?"

"Not a problem. I'll take the picture if you'll pick out Adrian Medina's baby picture and figure out where to put it."

"Oh, we got it?"

"His stepmom mailed us three pictures," Miss Wallace explained. "Wait until you see them! One with spaghetti or something all over his face."

Fred grabbed his camera and was about to hurry over to the gym. Christy caught him before he went out the door, and looking him in the eye, she said, "This is really nice of you, Fred. Thanks."

"Does this mean you'll go to the prom with me?"

"Fred!" Christy said, laughing.

"Never hurts to try." He gave her one of his toothy grins. "I do want to ask you something when I come back, though, okay?"

Christy felt a little nervous that he would put her on the spot for something. "You'd better hurry," she said. "You wouldn't want to have to try to assemble that bunch again."

"Right." Fred hustled out the door.

Christy went to work on the layout, playing with all the pictures and the copy as if it were a jigsaw puzzle. She didn't hear anyone come up behind her, but she then became aware that someone was looking over her shoulder. She turned around and saw Katie.

"That's Adrian?" Katie said, examining the photo of Adrian as a toddler splashing in a plastic kiddie pool that lay next to the one of him holding up the trophy the polo team had won this year. "He got his start in water sports early, I see."

"Cute, isn't it?" Christy said, feeling natural and at ease with Katie, as if no strain existed between them.

"Are you busy after school?" Katie asked.

"I don't think so." Christy knew work needed to be done on the yearbook, but then, the yearbook always needed work. She wasn't about to brush Katie off, since she apparently was now ready to talk.

"Can you meet me by my car? We'll grab a snack. My treat."

"Oh, well, if you're paying, then of course," Christy said with a smile.

Katie seemed to be fine. Maybe they wouldn't have that much to talk about. A few misunderstandings, some bruised feelings. Maybe they could move on from this point, and Christy would have a chance to really get to know Michael. Maybe she and Katie could renew their friendship and redeem what was left of their senior year.

Christy met Katie at her car right after school. Katie drove out of the parking lot in silence. Then they both began sentences at the same time.

"Oh, I'm sorry. Go ahead," Christy said.

"No, you go."

"I was just saying, so where do you want to go?"

"I thought you'd like to see my new hangout."

"Sure," Christy said. "And what were you going to say?"

"I was going to say it seems you're doing a good job on the yearbook and you really enjoy it."

"I do. I never would have guessed it would be so much fun. You know, I really only signed up because I needed one more class and, because I thought if I was on staff, I could make sure Fred didn't put in any of those embarrassing pictures like he did last year."

"Now you're the one putting in the embarrassing photos, so that makes it okay." The criticism in Katie's voice was evident.

"What do you mean?" Christy knew she sounded defensive.

"Nothing. Forget I said anything. That's not why I wanted to get together today. You have to do whatever you have to do. I'm not your judge. Too many people judge other people these days. Especially Christians."

Christy could guess what Katie was hinting at.

Silence ushered them down the main street of Escondido and sat beside them at a red light. When the light turned green, it was as if a signal went off, and both of them began to talk at the same time.

"We seem to be conversationally impaired today," Katie said, with her light laugh returning. "Here's the place."

She pulled into the driveway of a strip mall and parked in front of a small restaurant called The Organic Tomato.

"The Organic Tomato?" Christy asked.

"Don't worry. They serve a lot more than tomatoes," Katie said as she led Christy into the tiny cafe.

Christy struggled to believe this was Katie, the person who used to identify her four basic food groups as fat, sugar, preservatives and salt. Michael, who was into vitamins and health food, obviously was a powerful influence on Katie.

The small cafe was brightly lit. A dozen small, round tables with bright, flowered tablecloths were positioned around the room, making Christy feel as if she had stepped into a kaleidoscope. At any moment the tables might begin to spin, and she would be caught up in the swirl of repositioning colors. No one else was in the restaurant.

"Are you sure they're open?" Christy whispered.

"Oh, sure. Michael and I come here all the time after school." Katie walked to the back where a small window opened up to the kitchen.

"Hi, Janice. How's your day been?"

A slender, blonde woman with glowing skin and beautiful blue eyes stepped out, wearing an apron with a big red tomato on the front. "Great, Katie. How are you doing, Michael? Oh, that's not Michael."

"This is my friend Christy. Christy, this is Janice."

"Nice to meet you."

"And you."

"So what's your special for today?" Katie asked.

"It's the southwest tofu burger, with blue corn chips and fresh squeezed carrot juice."

Christy wasn't sure what all that was, but just hearing the

names made her want to gag. How could Katie stand this place?

"Sounds great," Katie said. "I'll have that. You want the same, Christy? Remember, it's my treat."

"Well, I was wondering if maybe I could see a menu."

"Sure," Janice said. "Here you go. There's a spinach and sprout salad you might like. The eggplant lasagna is also a favorite."

Christy nodded and accepted the flowery menu. She followed Katie to a table and said, "I had a lot for lunch. I was thinking of maybe just a soda."

"Soda?" Katie said.

Christy realized then that no one would walk into a place called The Organic Tomato and order a Coke.

"They have some all-natural sparkling beverages," Katie explained. "But mostly they serve juice. It's all squeezed fresh, right here."

"Oh, I'm sure it is," Christy said cautiously. "Maybe just an orange juice then."

"I heard," Janice called from the back. "Carrot juice and o.j. coming right up."

Christy didn't feel comfortable. It wasn't just the "organic" atmosphere. It was knowing that everything they said would he heard. Plus, none of the food on the menu even sounded familiar. At least she *thought* they were foods. Bulgar wheat salad, tofu scramble, lentil soup, bean curd. It looked as if a little kid had mixed up all the letters on the menu and put them back in the wrong places.

Janice appeared with the smallest glass of orange juice Christy had seen since she had ordered a kid's breakfast from Denny's a decade ago. The juice was so full of pulp she was tempted to use her spoon and eat it like soup. Somehow she thought that might upset Katie, so she took tiny sips and ran her tongue across her front teeth after every swallow, checking for stray pulp pieces.

Katie's tofu burger looked normal enough. Christy guessed the bun was made from organic, whole-grain something. It was a bit disturbing that the chips were a navy blue. But Christy decided that if she concentrated on Katie's face instead of her plate, she could pretend they were eating regular hamburgers and French fries at McDonald's like they used to before Katie met Michael.

"You want a bite?" Katie offered.

"No, thanks. I'm fine."

Katie took two or three bites and motioned for Christy to try a blue chip. She took a tiny one, and it tasted like a normal corn chip. Janice turned on some airy harp music, and Christy felt a little more at ease.

"God wants me to break up with Michael," Katie blurted out.

"Where did that come from?" Christy almost felt like laughing at Katie's abruptness.

"Please don't make light of this, Christy. I'm serious." Katie took another bite. Her expression grew sad. "And I've been disobeying God."

A dozen questions ran through Christy's mind. But she chose to remain silent and let Katie do the talking.

"I've known it for a couple of weeks now," Katie said. "All along I've been praying that Michael would surrender to the Lord. I thought that's why God brought him into my life, for me to show him how to become a Christian. And I've tried. Believe me! The six and a half months we've been together I've talked to him, given him books to read, taken him to Bible studies, introduced him to other Christians. And you know how I gave him that Bible for Christmas."

Christy nodded. She remembered shopping with Katie and looking at what seemed like every Bible ever made until Katie found one she thought Michael would read.

"He just won't believe. It's not that he can't believe that Christianity is the right way or that he doesn't believe in God, because he does. It's that he won't surrender his life to Christ."

Christy could see the pain in Katie's eyes.

"I told God that if He wanted me to break up with Michael, I would. And then God told me to break up with him. Don't ask me how I know. Michael wanted to know how God talks to me. I can't explain it. It's just that deep inside my heart I know what the Holy Spirit is telling me."

Katie took another bite of her burger and motioned for Christy to have another chip. She obliged.

"So two weeks ago when you saw us in the school parking lot, I had just told Michael. I said we had to break up."

"Oh, Katie, I didn't know."

"That was the thing. See, on the way back to school I prayed for a sign. I know you're not supposed to mess with God like that, but I was so upset. I said, "God, if I did the right thing by breaking up with Michael, then make me run into Christy on the way home.""

"You're kidding."

"No. It was such a God thing, I couldn't believe it. When I prayed that, I knew you would either be working at the pet store or on the yearbook. Then there you were, standing by my car! After that I don't know what happened. Michael said some mean things, and I got really mad at God because He was making me do this."

Katie waved her hand at Christy's confused expression. "I know, it's dumb, but it was like God did what I asked by putting you there, and then I got mad. I couldn't even talk to you."

"Yes, I noticed," Christy said softly.

"It was as if you were on God's side, and somehow you were both against me. I don't know, Christy. I was a mess for a couple of days. Then Michael and I got back together. He's happy. I'm happy. Everything is normal, except I know I'm disobeying God. So I'm ignoring Him." Katie chomped into her burger and ate silently for a moment.

"Why are you talking to me now?" Christy asked. "Does it seem like I'm not on God's side any more?"

"No!" Katie said quickly. "You are. That's why I thought I needed to talk to you face to face. I want you to tell me to break up with Michael."

"I can't do that," Christy said. "That's between you and God and Michael."

"Thanks a lot," Katie muttered.

"What do you mean?"

"I mean, all along you kept warning me about him not being a Christian, and now that I want you to tell me to break up, you won't do it."

"I can't," Christy said. Then using Michael's words, she added, "I haven't earned the right. I'm not your personal Holy Spirit. You have to listen to what God tells you to do and then choose to obey or disobey."

"I'm disobeying," Katie admitted sadly. "It's a creepy feeling."

"Then why don't you break up with him for good this time?"

"There's only one problem."

"What's that?"

"I'm in love with him."

CHAPTER THREE

Blessed Are the Peacemakers

"You're in love with him," Christy repeated. "What does that mean?"

"It means," Katie said, putting down her burger, "I'm in love with him. Do you know how hard it is to push someone out of your life when you're in love with him? It's impossible! Christy, there has never been any other guy in my life. There might never be any others! For six months the center of my universe has been Michael, and it's been wonderful. Why would I give that up?"

"Because God told you to?" Christy ventured.

"Exactly! But I want a human to tell me so I'll know it's the right thing to do. You have to help me out here, Christy."

Christy remained silent, confused as to what to say. It would be easier if she could have time to think all this through. Would it be okay for her to go ahead and say, "Yes, Katie, God has told me to tell you to break up with Michael?" Or should she stick with her gut feeling that this was a decision Katie had to make, with or without a cheering section?

"You're not going to help me on this one, are you, Christy?"

"Katie, you already know what I think about all this. I think Michael is a great guy, and he's been the perfect boyfriend for you. But unless he becomes a Christian, the only areas you have in common are the emotional and physical. The spiritual part of you will never connect with him, and that's the part of you that's going to last forever."

"You sound like Todd," Katie said.

Christy took that as a compliment.

"So go ahead, Christy, finish your speech. Tell me what to do."

Christy hesitated. "Katie," she said firmly, "you have to do what God tells you to."

"You make me so mad!" Katie spouted, pushing away her plate. "You have no idea how hard this is, Christy."

"I know," Christy said softly.

"No, you don't!" Katie yelled. "You've never gone through anything like this. This is the hardest thing I've ever done. I love him, yet I'm breaking up with him because God told me to! That's the only reason. Do you have any idea how stupid that sounds to Michael? All that witnessing. All those books. All those Bible studies. And now I'm telling him God is so mean that He won't let us go out anymore!"

Christy didn't know what to say.

"Come on," Katie said. "Let's get out of here." She left enough money on the table to cover the meal and marched out to the car. Christy hurried after her and jumped in just as Katie backed up sharply and swerved into the flow of traffic. "God is so totally unfair!"

Christy grabbed onto the side of her seat as a car cut in front of them. Katie laid on the horn and yelled, "Why did God bring Michael into my life only to jerk him away? I am so mad right now I could scream!" And Katie promptly screamed.

Christy had always admired Katie's ability to express her feelings. But she had never seen Katie this upset.

Katie sped into the school parking lot and pulled up next to Christy's car with a screech.

"Are you okay?" Christy asked before getting out.

"No, of course not. What a stupid question! I'm dying here, Christy. Have a little sympathy, will you?"

"What can I do?" Christy felt flustered.

"Nothing. I asked you for help, and you wouldn't give it to me. If I'm going to do this, I'm going to have to do it without any human affirmation. So just leave me alone."

"Do you want to call me later?" Christy asked.

"Maybe."

"Call me," Christy urged, hopping out of the car. She wasn't sure Katie heard her, because Katie started to speed away just as Christy closed the door.

Christy felt awful as she drove home. Her stomach didn't seem to like the pulpy orange juice, plus a flood of accusations swept over her.

You're a terrible friend, Christy. You're so chicken, you couldn't even tell Katie the right thing to do. All you could do was hide behind God and force Katie to make her own decision. Is that the compassionate, Christian thing to do?

The minute Christy arrived home, she grabbed the phone and called Todd. To her relief, he answered on the first ring. Christy spilled out all the events of the past hour.

"You did the right thing," Todd said. "Don't listen to all those doubts and accusations. Those aren't coming from the Lord. You pushed Katie closer to God. You made her responsible for her choice. You did the right thing."

"Then how come I feel so terrible?"

"Maybe because you would like everything to be smooth and easy, and it isn't always like that. You're a peacemaker, Christy. I like that about you. God says the peacemakers will be called His sons and daughters. How do you feel about that? Christy Miller, daughter of the King! Should I start calling you Princess now?"

Christy let out a gentle laugh. "Only if you want me to call you Prince Todd."

"I can live with that."

"Well, Prince Todd, thanks for listening. You're a peacemaker for me, I hope you know. I appreciate you so much. Thanks for always being there."

"You're welcome, Princess. So what do you want to do this weekend?"

"I don't know. Should I see if I can get off on Saturday and stay at my Uncle Bob and Aunt Marti's? You and I could spend some time on the beach." Christy's imagination began to swirl with dreams of walking hand in hand on Newport Beach at sunset.

"Sounds good to me. Call me after you figure it all out."

"Okay, I will. Thanks again, Todd. I don't know what I'd do without you."

"You would probably be closer to God, because you would have to talk to Him more," Todd said. Then with a quick "Later," he hung up.

What did Todd mean by that? Does he think I don't talk to God very much or that I'm not close to God? Oh, well. I'm not going to worry about it. One thing Todd is right about, I do like things calm and peaceful. Looking for hidden meanings in his words does not make me feel peaceful!

Christy quickly dialed her aunt and uncle's phone number. They lived only a few blocks from Todd's dad in Newport Beach, and over the past few years Todd had become like a son to them. There should be no problem inviting herself to visit for the weekend. But the answering machine picked up her call on the fourth ring. She left a message and then called Jon, her boss at the pet store.

"Hi, Jon. It's Christy. I wanted to see if I could have Saturday off."

"Saturday, as in the day after tomorrow?"

"Yes."

"You're asking me now? And you think I should give you the whole day off?"

"Yes." Christy thought she knew Jon well enough to know he was teasing her. At least she thought he was teasing her.

"Big date with Todd?" Jon asked.

"Well, kind of. I'm probably going to go up to Newport for the weekend. I could work another evening next week if you need me to make up the hours."

"No, it's okay. You haven't had any time off for the past few months. I'd say you're ready for a break. You'll still be here tomorrow for your regular hours, won't you?"

"Yes, of course. Thanks, Jon. Did anyone ever tell you what a nice boss you are?"

"No," Jon said plainly.

"Then let me be the first. You're a very nice boss, Jon!"

"You don't have to schmooze me anymore, Christy. I already said you could have the day off."

"I know, but I might want to ask another favor someday."

"Well, next time I'll say no."

"Thanks for saying yes this time, Jon. I'll see you tomorrow."

The minute Christy hung up the phone, it rang again. Startled, she jumped and then answered it.

"Okay," the voice on the other end said. "I did it. It's for good this time. Now I'm going to go crazy. I am absolutely going to go crazy!"

"Katie," Christy said cautiously, "tell me what happened."

"I went right over to his house and told Michael that I loved him, but I had to break up with him, and the only reason was because I knew that's what God was telling me to do. He said, 'You know that I love you, Katie, and now I love you more, because you're one of the few women I know who would make such a decision because of her convictions.' Then he kissed me on the cheek, and I ran out the door."

Christy could tell that Katie was crying. She let Katie sob a few moments before trying to comfort her.

"You did the right thing, Katie."

"Then why does it hurt so bad?"

"I guess the good feelings don't always come in the same envelope as the right answer."

Katie burst out laughing. "Did you hear yourself? What is that supposed to mean?"

"It's the first thing that popped into my head. What I mean is, for now, all you can know is that you did the right thing. I think the feelings will catch up eventually."

"I hope you're right. I can't believe I did it. I'm going to hate myself tomorrow. Oh, no," Katie groaned. "Tomorrow is Friday. What am I going to do?"

"What do you mean?" Christy asked.

"For the past six months Michael and I have always been together on the weekends. I have to have something else to do. Promise me you'll spend the whole weekend with me, Christy. I'll go crazy if I'm by myself."

"Well, I . . ."

"I know you have to work, but that's okay. I'll go to work with you. I'm sure Jon can find something for me to do in the back room. He doesn't have to pay me or anything. I just can't stay home by myself."

"Sure," Christy said boldly. "We'll work something out. I was trying to make plans to go to Bob and Marti's. I'm sure they wouldn't mind if you came, too."

"Oh," Katie said, sounding depressed. "You probably wanted to be with Todd. You don't need me in the way."

"No, Katie, it's fine. Really. You know Todd; he won't mind a bit. I'd love to spend the weekend with you. It's been so long since we've done anything together. It'll be great. You'll see."

"Well, if you're sure."

"Yes, I'm sure. I'll give my aunt another call, and then I'll call you back. You might as well start packing, Katie. I'm sure it'll work out."

"I broke up with Michael." Katie sounded like she couldn't believe her own statement. "I really did it. I broke up with him for good."

"Katie, are you okay?"

"No," Katie said somberly. "But I will be. Someday. Not tomorrow. But one day, I will be. Call me back. Bye."

Christy listened to the dial tone and wondered if Katie really would be okay. She hung up and tried to sort out all the events of the past few hours. After weeks—no months—of stifled tension between Katie and her, in the last two and a half hours everything had changed.

In a way, Christy wished Katie's big breakup with Michael hadn't come until Monday. That way, at least Christy and Todd could have had a fun weekend together. The minute she thought it, she felt bad.

She and Todd had enjoyed months of terrific weekends together, and during many of those weekends they had discussed

Katie and Michael's relationship. Over and over Todd had told Christy to wait and be patient, to stick with Katie through this whole thing. He had told her there was a time for everything. Apparently now was the time for Christy to come alongside Katie and support her and cry along with her. Todd would understand.

And he did. When she called him later that evening to tell him that she had reached Bob and Marti and they were delighted to have Katie and Christy come up for the weekend, Todd said, "I'll see if Doug can come home from college this weekend. We'll all have to go to Disneyland or something."

"That would be fun," Christy agreed. "You know, you and I haven't been to Disneyland since our very first date. When was that? Three years ago?"

"Yeah, I'd say it's time we go again. Doug's great when it comes to cheering up brokenhearted women. He'll be a good companion for Katie."

"Doug doesn't have a girlfriend yet?" Christy asked. "I thought he would have met somebody by now."

"Nope. He told me once that he thought he knew whom God wanted him to marry, but he was waiting for the girl to figure it out. He wouldn't tell me who it was."

"You think it might be Tracy?" Christy asked. "They went out for a while."

"I don't know. He wouldn't give me any hints. Could be Katie, for all we know. Doesn't matter, though. Doug's sure that God will work it all out."

"I guess Katie and I will drive up together on Friday night as soon as I get off work. We'll get to Bob and Marti's after ten. Is that too late for you guys? I mean, do you want to get together on Friday night, or wait and do something on Saturday?"

"Whatever," Todd said amiably. "We'll take it as it comes."

"I'm looking forward to seeing you," Christy said softly.

"Yeah, I'm looking forward to seeing you, too."

"Bye," Christy said.

"Later."

Christy made a quick phone call to Katie and filled her in on the plans. Even though Katie sounded tired at first, she spoke up when Christy mentioned Doug.

"I don't want charity," Katie said. "Doug is not interested in me, he never has been, he never will be. I don't want him coming along just to give me all his little hugs and try to make me feel better."

"Okay, fine. Doug might not even come. But we're still going to Disneyland, and that will be fun," Christy said, trying to sound cheerful.

"Yeah, right. You, Todd, and me. What a fun day that will be. Is Todd going to hold hands with both of us so I won't feel left out?"

Christy was beginning to get irritated. "Katie, will you stop it? We're going to the pet store tomorrow after school, and then you and I are going to drive up to Newport, stay at my aunt and uncle's, probably go to Disneyland on Saturday and then church with Todd on Sunday, and you are going to have a wonderful time. Got it?"

"Sorry," Katie said. "I'll try not to be a brat this weekend. I appreciate your making room for me in your plans."

"It'll be fun, Katie. You'll see. I'm really looking forward to it."

"Me too," Katie said with a sigh. "I wonder what Michael is going to do this weekend? I guess it doesn't matter, does it?"

Christy didn't answer.

"Well," Katie said, snapping back to a more positive tone of voice, "I have some more homework to finish. I'll see you to-morrow. Thanks again, Christy. This is the true test of a best friend. Thanks for sticking with me through all this."

"There's nothing to thank me for, Katie. I'll see you after school. Good night."

Christy hung up, thinking, *If you only knew how selfish I'm feeling right now about having to share Todd with you this weekend, you wouldn't be thanking me.*

CHAPTER FOUR

Just Let Me Hurt

"Oh, Miss Chris," Fred said the minute Christy walked into yearbook class on Friday. "May I have a moment of your time?"

"What do you want, Fred?" Christy was not in the mood to deal with him.

"Do you remember yesterday, right before I left to take the photo of the volleyball team, I said I wanted to talk to you about something?"

Christy didn't remember, but she wanted to speed this conversation along, so she nodded and waited for Fred's reply, expecting another invitation to the prom.

"I wanted to ask you something."

"What, Fred?" she said, her irritation showing.

"I wanted to ask you what church you went to."

"Why?" Christy asked, surprised.

"I kind of wanted to try going sometime."

"Why?" Christy asked, and the minute she did, she realized how rude she sounded.

"It's a free country," Fred said, puffing out his chest a little. "At least, the last time I checked, it was. I've never been to church before. I thought I might like to try it sometime."

"That's great, Fred," Christy said, quickly changing her tone. "I think you'll like it. It's a really good church." She gave him directions and specifics on when the high school group met and when church services were held.

"Thanks," Fred said. "I'll see you there this Sunday."

"Oh," Christy said, "is that why you wanted to go to church? Just because I do?"

"No!" Fred answered defensively.

"Well, I'm not going to be there this Sunday. I'm going to be at my aunt and uncle's for the weekend." Then, trying to sound nice, she added, "Some other people from school go there, though, so I'm sure you'll see somebody you know."

"Like Katie," Fred said.

"Actually, Katie is going to be with me. There are other people, though. I think you'll like it; you should go."

"I will," Fred said. "Are you ready to work on these last two collage pages with me? We have to have everything done by next Wednesday. That's the final, final, drop dead deadline."

"Are you sure?"

"Yes, I'm sure."

Christy couldn't help but wonder about Fred's interest in attending church. She would have liked to believe he was becoming interested in Christianity. Maybe somehow she had been a witness to him, although she wasn't sure how. Most of the year she had been rude to him, and she had never tried talking to him about spiritual things. Somehow, she couldn't help but wonder if it was one of his tactics to spend time with her, especially since they would be done with their mutual projects by next Wednesday. They wouldn't have too many other reasons to talk to each other after the yearbook was done. That is, unless Fred started going to her church.

She told Katie about it on the way to work after school that afternoon. It had been months since Katie and Christy had talked like this, and Katie said she didn't even know Fred had been chasing Christy.

"Only all year," Christy said.

"Man," Katie said with a sigh, "we've missed a lot this year, haven't we? I mean, our whole senior year is almost over, and you and I barely know what's going on with each other."

"I know," Christy said.

"I regret that, Christy, and I know it's all my fault because I was so wrapped up in Michael."

"It's not all your fault. I didn't exactly make things comfortable for either of us. I could have done a lot more to keep our friendship close, but I didn't. I'm sorry I didn't try harder."

"Let's promise each other that we'll never do that again," Katie said, looking solemn. "Let's promise that we'll never in our whole lives let a guy come between us. Even when we're old and senile, we'll still be best friends."

"Promise," Christy said. "Although, if I'm senile, I can't promise that I'll exactly remember who you are from day to day."

"Then we'll just have to make sure they check us both into a rest home where all the patients wear name tags," Katie said, and the two friends laughed together—something they hadn't done for months.

The evening at the pet store zipped by. Christy had quietly let Jon know that Katie and Michael had broken up, and Jon made sure Katie kept busy in the stock room, helping him rearrange supplies. Jon kept her laughing, too, with all his stories about crazy customers.

Just as the two girls were about to leave the store, Christy sidled up to Jon and said, "Remind me to do something nice for you someday."

Jon smiled and whispered, "She's not through the worst of it yet. It'll hit her pretty hard. Probably sometime this weekend. Anyone who's had a broken heart knows it gets worse before it gets better."

Jon's expression and tender words made Christy wonder who had once broken his heart. Maybe he had never recovered, since he was in his early thirties and still not married.

"You want ice cream or frozen yogurt or something before the long drive up to Newport Beach?" Christy asked as she and Katie headed for the car. "We could stop by Baskin-Robbins on our way out of town."

Katie didn't answer.

Christy unlocked the passenger door, and Katie got in, fastened her seat belt, and looked straight ahead, as if in a daze.

"Hello, Earth to Katie. Do you want to stop by 31 Flavors or not?" Christy asked. Then she noticed a stream of tears pouring down Katie's cheeks.

"That's the first place we ever went together. Remember? It was the day we met. Right after school, I told Michael I was going to educate him on how many vitamins could be found in a scoop of Jamoca Almond Fudge ice cream."

Christy swallowed hard. Things had been going so well at work. She hadn't expected this kind of sorrow attack. "We don't have to stop there. We don't have to stop anywhere. We can just drive straight to Bob and Marti's. Forget I suggested it. Bad suggestion."

Maneuvering the car out of the parking lot, Christy checked Katie's face each time they passed a street light to see if the tears were letting up.

"Do you realize," Christy said, "this is the first time since we went to San Diego about this time last year that you and I have gone anywhere together, just the two of us? And can you believe my parents actually let me take the car for the whole weekend? This is really a first, Katie."

Katie leaned back against the headrest and closed her eyes. In a choked voice she said, "Take me home, Christy. I can't do this."

"Sure you can," Christy said cheerfully. "We're going to have a great time together this weekend. You'll forget all about Michael."

"I don't want to forget about Michael!" Katie said, raising her voice. "There are no bad memories to try to forget. Everything was wonderful. You don't get it, do you? I loved him. I still love him!"

Christy drove silently onto the freeway and moved into the middle lane. They passed the off-ramp for Katie's house, but Katie said nothing. Christy assumed Katie didn't really want to go home. She just needed to get away. Christy decided it was up to her to convince Katie that they were going to have a good time.

Christy drove a little faster. The farther Katie got from home, the less realistic it would be for them to turn around and go back, and the more enthusiastic she might become about the weekend.

They continued in silence. Christy felt relieved that traffic was light. They should make it to Bob and Marti's in about an hour and a half. She wondered if she should turn on the radio. No, a song might come on that would remind Katie of Michael, although Christy didn't know what song that might be. She realized how little she knew about Michael and Katie and the things that were special to them. Maybe they should talk about anything unrelated to Michael.

"Did I tell you we have until Wednesday to finish up everything on the yearbook? I think it turned out really well. It's been a lot of fun. Maybe I'll take some courses like that in college. That reminds me. I never heard what you decided about college next year. Did you hear back from any of the ones you applied to?"

Katie pursed her lips. "I was accepted at the Queens University in Belfast. That's where Michael is going next year."

"Belfast? You mean in Ireland? I didn't know you even applied. Are you still going there? What am I saying? Of course you're not. What's your next choice?"

"I don't know," Katie said. "I didn't have any backup plans."

Christy could see the tears starting to slide down Katie's freckled cheeks again. She knew she'd better start talking fast. "I guess I'm going to Palomar Community College, at least for my freshman year. My aunt wants me to go to a state university. You know they started a college savings account for me several years ago. Well, there's probably enough for my first year. But my parents think I should wait until I have a better idea of what I want my major to be before I go to a university. That way I can get all the general ed. courses out of the way. Palomar is pretty good, from what I hear. Why don't you go to Palomar with me? It'd be great, Katie. We could even take some classes together."

By now they were well on their way down the freeway and were driving past Camp Pendleton Marine Corps Base. Katie stared blankly out the window.

"Maybe I'll join the army," Katie mumbled.

"The army?" Christy questioned with a laugh.

"All right, then, the air force."

"Katie, you crack me up," Christy said. "You belong in a drama class."

"I'm not being dramatic," Katie said, facing Christy. Katie's eyes looked puffy in the dim light.

"What I mean is, you seem like you would be great as the star in a school play. I can see you going to college and majoring in acting much more than I picture you in the cockpit of a fighter plane."

"Acting, huh?" Katie said.

"I think you would be great in drama. You have a natural flare for it. I always said you would be the next Lucille Ball."

"I don't feel like I'm going to be the next anything. I hurt so bad, Christy. You can't imagine how bad this hurts."

"That's because you keep thinking about it. Try to get your mind on something else. Let's play a game or something. I know. I'm thinking of an animal that starts with the letter 'G.' "

"It's giraffe, and I don't want to play."

"How did you know it was a giraffe?"

"You pick a giraffe first every time we play this stupid game."

"Okay," Christy said, still trying to move the conversation off Michael, "your turn. You pick one."

"Christy," Katie said sharply, "you don't get it, do you? I don't want to play any stupid games. I'm hurting. Just let me hurt, will you!"

Christy recoiled, trying hard not to let her wounded feelings show. Now *she* was the one who wanted to turn around and take Katie home. With Katie so set on feeling sorry for herself, it was bound to be a miserable weekend.

If only Katie and Michael hadn't broken up. What am I thinking? I prayed for this for months, and now I wish she was still with him? I'm so confused! What am I supposed to say to cheer her up? I can't understand why she's hurting so much—she did the right thing, and she knows it.

"Katie," Christy began softly, "you're right. I don't totally understand what you're feeling. I'm trying to say the right things here, and I don't seem to be helping at all. Maybe you can help me understand. I mean, you broke up with Michael because you were convinced God told you to break up with him. Tell me what you're feeling now."

Katie shook her head. "There's no way of explaining it. It's like a death, Christy, a loss of something precious. It doesn't matter how prepared you are for that death, it still hurts. It just really, really hurts."

"I'm sorry," Christy said. "I wish I could do something."

"Just let me hurt."

Christy remembered a conversation she had had with Todd several weeks ago after Katie had acted so strangely in the school parking lot. Todd's advice had been to release her and wait. What was that other part he had said about the true test of love? Something about how the strength of love is when you can let go.

Katie showed incredible strength when she let go of Michael. Now it was Christy's turn to let go of her goal of making Katie feel happy. If Katie needed to feel sad for a while, then she needed to be released by Christy to feel sad.

Biting her lower lip, Christy determined to try to understand what would be best for Katie, to somehow release her and not take her angry words personally.

"Okay," Christy said, "I'm trying to understand. I want you to know that you're free to feel whatever you feel and say whatever you want to say around me. I know I won't always understand it all, but I want to try. So please don't think you have to act a certain way this weekend. Just be whatever you need to be. And I promise I'll stop trying to cheer you up."

"Thanks, Chris," Katie said, releasing a giant sigh. "I don't want to mess up this weekend for you and Todd."

"You won't. Besides, it's our weekend, too—yours and mine.

And you need to be free to feel whatever you're going to feel."

"I hope you never go through this, Christy. You can't imagine how powerful your emotions can be. I think I'd rather have my toenails pulled out one by one by an army of ferocious snapping turtles."

Christy laughed, and Katie cracked a smile.

"I don't know why," Katie said, "but I feel a little better."

"Good," Christy said, flashing Katie a comforting smile.

When they arrived at Bob and Marti's, Todd's old VW bus, Gus, was parked in the driveway. Christy felt warmed inside just knowing he was there waiting for her.

The girls hauled their weekend luggage to the front door and were met with a round of hugs from Todd, Doug, Bob, and Marti. To Christy it seemed like a "welcome home" party. Katie looked a little wary, as if she were suspicious of everyone's warm affections.

"You ladies hungry? Something to drink, perhaps?" Uncle Bob, always the gracious host, looked as if he had just come from the golf course. He had on a light blue knit shirt, khaki shorts, and white deck shoes with no socks. For a man in his early fifties who had never had children, he looked and acted like one of the college boys.

"Sure," Christy said, "I could go for something. How about you, Katie?"

Marti, Christy's petite aunt, grasped Katie's arm with her long, perfectly manicured nails and said, "I heard you've become quite the healthy eater. I'm so pleased! Wait until you see what I bought just for you and me this weekend." Marti led Katie through the swinging door into the kitchen, and the rest of them followed.

"Look!" Marti said with glee. "Organic carrots that I just ran through my juicer." She poured a tall glass of the thick, very orange juice and handed it to Katie.

Katie graciously accepted and lifted the glass to her lips. Christy felt shivers just looking at the gloppy juice. She didn't know how Katie could manage to drink it.

Katie took a sip and said, "It's very good, Marti. Thanks."

Christy thought she detected tears glistening in Katie's puffy eyes.

"Here, Christy," Marti said, pouring another glass. "You'll have to try some."

"I really don't think I can, Aunt Marti. Thanks, but I'd like a glass of water, if that's okay."

Marti looked disappointed, but only for a moment before she turned her attention back to Katie, who had taken another swig of the juice. "I have spinach quiche for us for breakfast, and tomorrow for lunch I'll make you some of my jicama, alfalfa sprout, and currant salad. You'll love it."

"Don't go to any trouble on my account," Katie said.

"Are you kidding? This is a dream come true for me! I've been trying to get Christy to eat like this for years. Goodness knows, Robert will never try my food. I'm thrilled to have someone to share my recipes with."

"And if you get tired of rabbit food," Bob said with a twinkle in his eye, "you can share my recipes for some real food like donuts, bean dip, and pork chops."

"And that's just for breakfast," Doug said, and they all laughed.

Doug was the kind of guy who seemed to always be in a good mood. Tall, with sandy blond hair and a little boy smile, he was famous for his big hugs.

Christy was laughing until she looked over at Katie. Katie had placed the half-empty glass on the counter, and now tears were trickling down her face. She quickly wiped them with the back of her hand and blinked away their companions. Then, with her head down, she quietly slipped out of the kitchen.

"Is she all right?" Marti asked. "It wasn't something I said, was it?"

"No, she's okay. She's just hurting," Christy said.

"Well, then, go after her and cheer her up!" Marti said.

"I already tried that," Christy said. "I think she just needs to be alone for a bit. She'll be okay."

"Why don't I take her things up to her room," Bob offered and left the kitchen.

The rest of them stood in silence, looking at each other. None of them seemed to know what to do or say.

"She'll be okay," Christy repeated. "She'll be better tomorrow."

Christy could only hope she was right.

CHAPTER FIVE

The Happiest Place on Earth

At 8:45 the next morning, Todd, Doug, Christy, and Katie piled into Gus the Bus and cheerfully waved good-bye to Bob and Marti.

"Say hi to Mickey Mouse for me," Bob called out.

"I'll save the rest of the spinach quiche for when you come home, Katie," Marti said.

Todd popped Gus into gear, and they sputtered down the road.

"Boy, does this feel like a time warp," Christy said, reaching over and giving Todd's arm a squeeze. "Remember the last time you took me to Disneyland, and Bob and Marti sent us off?"

"I still remember what Bob said," Todd replied with a grin that made his dimple appear. " 'Have fun. I won't worry about you unless it's after midnight and we haven't heard from you yet.' I thought for sure you would turn into a pumpkin if I didn't have you back by midnight!"

"All I remember is that Tracy was sitting right here," Christy said, pointing to where she sat in the front seat. "And I thought you had invited her to go with us, but you were only giving her a ride to work."

"That's right," Todd said, looking as if it was hard for him to remember that part.

"I felt horrible because I snapped at Tracy, and then she sweetly handed me a birthday present."

"What was it?" Katie asked.

"My Bible. It was actually from Todd and Tracy, but she made the fabric cover on it."

"I never knew that," Katie said. "A lot of Christians were nice to you before you came to know the Lord, weren't they?"

Christy interpreted that as a little jab that she hadn't been nicer to Michael. She realized Katie was right. She was about to answer with an apology when Todd stopped at a red light. He hopped out of the van and jogged around to Christy's door.

"What's he doing?" Katie asked.

Christy couldn't answer but let out a bubble of delighted laughter. This was their intersection. This was where Todd had first kissed her and where he had given her the gold "Forever" ID bracelet she wore on her right wrist. Todd opened Christy's door, and practically scooping her up in his arms, he helped her out of the van. Together they ran to the front of the vehicle, and in front of Doug and Katie and the whole world, Todd wrapped his arms around Christy and quickly kissed her. Then he let go as fast as he had embraced her, and they each ran to their side of Gus and hopped in just as the light turned green. Todd slid the van from neutral to first gear and drove on as if nothing unusual had happened.

"So how about those Dodgers?" Doug said to Katie.

"I don't see anybody doing any dodging," Katie quipped back.

Doug laughed and kept laughing all the way down the freeway to Anaheim. Christy realized the little encounter at the intersec-

tion was probably embarrassing for Katie and Doug, but to
Christy it meant everything. It meant that Todd valued their special memories as much as she did and that he didn't care if the
whole world knew they were going together. It was a wonderful,
warm, delicious feeling, and Christy hoped it would last all day.

They parked Gus and took the tram to Disneyland's entrance.
Christy had her camera looped over her arm and a sweatshirt
wrapped around her waist.

That morning she had remembered the peach-colored T-shirt
she had worn on her first Disneyland date with Todd and wished
she had brought it to wear just for the memories. Instead, she had
on a cream-colored T-shirt and jeans. Katie wore jeans, too, and
a green cotton shirt. Both the guys had on shorts, and they all
had brought along sweatshirts for the cool of the evening. Their
first stop inside the park was at the lockers to leave their sweatshirts.

"Where to first?" Doug asked. "I'm a Tomorrowland kind of
guy. You might as well all know that right up front."

"What I hear you saying," Todd said, "is that Space Mountain is calling your name. Am I right?"

"What can I say? I have the need for speed."

"My kind of guy," Katie said, flashing Doug a big smile.

Christy's stomach started to feel a little queasy, thinking
about all the roller coaster rides these three would want to go on.
She preferred the gentle boat rides like It's a Small, Small World.
Last time Todd had talked her into the bobsleds, and that was
about the wildest ride she had ever been on. Apparently, it was
tame compared to some of these others.

"Tomorrowland it is," Todd said. "As long as we make it to
Adventureland before it's dark, I'll be happy."

"My favorite is Thunder Mountain," Katie said.

She had been doing a great job of keeping cheerful all morning. Perhaps letting her alone last night to cry herself to sleep had been the best thing for her.

"What's your favorite, Christy?" Katie asked.

She didn't dare say It's a Small, Small World, so she said the first thing that came to her mind. "I like the Swiss Family Robinson Tree House."

Todd stopped walking and looked at Christy with pleased surprise. "Really? That's cool." Then he took her hand and gave it a squeeze.

"She just said that because she knows it's your favorite spot, Todd," Doug said over his shoulder. He and Katie were leading the way, blazing the trail down Main Street as they headed toward Tomorrowland.

If she had thought about it, Christy would have remembered how Todd had turned into a free-spirited Tarzan in the tree house when they had climbed through it on their first visit here. Todd's dream was no secret to anybody who knew him well. He wanted to be a missionary and live off the land in a jungle somewhere. He had never wavered from that goal, and more than once Christy had questioned whether or not she had what it took to be a missionary as well.

Fortunately, that question didn't need to be answered for a long time. For now, she and Todd were together. Things had never been better. She had never been happier.

The line for Space Mountain was long, and they had to wait about forty minutes before it was their turn. But the time went fast, with Katie and Doug chattering away.

Christy was relieved to see Katie doing so well emotionally. Doug was a great encourager. If anyone could make Katie feel better, it was Doug. Good ol' Doug. Christy decided she was going

to try and find some way to let him know how much she appreciated him.

Soon they were stepping into the cars that would take them
whirling through the darkness on this inside roller coaster.
Christy climbed in and immediately curled up against Todd's
chest. He circled her with his arms and whispered, "Scaredy-
cat?"

Christy answered with a little "meow" just as the car lurched
forward and the ride began. Squeezing her eyes shut, she clung
to Todd's arm and clenched her jaw to keep from screaming. She
could hear Katie shrieking and Doug laughing from the seats in
front of them. She wondered how many other adrenaline-pump-
ing rides they would coax her onto before the day was over.

The answer was five. They went on every fast ride they could
find. The only comforting part was that each time she could cud-
dle up with Todd, close her eyes, and feel his strong arms around
her. She had never felt this close to him before. It was as if Todd
was sheltering her, protecting her, and letting her lean on him for
strength. She wondered if he felt the closeness, too.

Each time they stepped off one of the wild rides, Christy kept
her arm around Todd's waist. She wanted to feel his arms circling
her all day. All week. All year. The rest of her life. This was where
she belonged.

"Anyone hungry besides me?" Doug asked around noon.

"I think your stomach has a timer," Katie said. "It goes off
about every hour, doesn't it? I mean, it couldn't be much more
than an hour since you had that popcorn."

"Hey, I'm a growing boy," Doug said.

"I'm just giving you a hard time," Katie said. "I'm hungry,
too. What do you guys want to eat?"

They were near the center of the park, by Sleeping Beauty's

Castle. Todd suggested they grab a hamburger at the Carnation Plaza.

"Did you know they have Fantasia ice cream here?" Doug asked as they stood in line to order their hamburgers a few minutes later. "I think this is the only place in the world you can get it."

"What is it?" Katie asked.

"It's kind of hard to describe. It has maraschino cherries in it and other stuff."

"Did you know there's enough red dye in a jar of maraschino cherries to kill a laboratory test rat?" Katie asked. The minute she said it, everyone looked at her, including people standing in the line next to them. "At least, that's what I've heard," she said in an apologetic way.

It was her turn to order at the small window. Katie asked the girl in the striped apron if they had whole wheat buns.

"No, sorry."

"Okay, well, this is what I want. I want a hamburger with extra tomatoes, lettuce, pickles, and onions and no meat."

"No meat?" the girl asked. "I think it's still the same price."

"That's okay," Katie said.

"Hey," Doug said, sliding in next to Katie and bending to address the girl inside, "put her hamburger patty on mine. I'll eat her meat."

"I'm not sure we can do that. Maybe you two could swap your own meat."

"Fine with me," Doug said.

"Okay," Katie agreed. "Are your french fries prepared in pure vegetable oil by any chance?"

"Are they what?" the girl asked.

"Never mind," Katie said. "No french fries. Just the burger with all the extras."

Once they had ordered and found a place to sit, Christy thought she noticed a cloud beginning to form over Katie's countenance. Did her attempt to order healthy food make her think too much about Michael?

"Slap that baby right here," Doug said, opening the bun of his double cheeseburger and waiting for Katie to slip her meat inside. "You want my tomatoes?"

"Sure," Katie said. "I'll take your lettuce, too, if you don't want it. I don't care about the pickles."

Doug swapped his lettuce and tomatoes for Katie's hamburger. She patted the top of her "veggie burger," looking pleased with the trade.

"Don't they remind you of a nursery rhyme couple?" Todd asked Christy. "You know, that one about the Jack guy who couldn't eat any fat and his wife who was totally into carbohydrates. Only these guys have it in reverse."

"Katie just doesn't know what's good for her," Doug said. He lifted his bulging burger up to her mouth and said, "Come on, just one little bite. You can't go organic the rest of your life."

Katie turned her head away and playfully said, "Get that thing away from me, Michael."

The instant she said "Michael," everything stopped.

"I mean, Doug," Katie said sheepishly, her bottom lip beginning to quiver.

"Hey, that's okay," Doug said calmly.

Christy could tell that Katie was trying not to cry, but it seemed impossible for her to hold back the tears. Doug's tender words were equivalent to the thumb of the little boy plugging the great sea wall in Holland. Perhaps Doug realized that, because he pulled his chair over next to Katie's and putting his arms around her, he offered her his broad chest to cry on.

"Go ahead," Doug said, gently pulling Katie closer. "You can cry. It's okay. Go ahead."

Christy thought Katie would pull away, but to her surprise, Katie fell into Doug's embrace and began to cry. Actually, she began to wail like Christy had never heard anyone cry before. She glanced around, aware that they had an audience of all the tourists sitting close to them in this open air patio. Dozens of people who thought they were spending their day at "The Happiest Place on Earth" seemed dying to know what was wrong with the wailing redhead.

"Come here," Doug said, tenderly helping Katie to her feet while her face was still smashed against his chest. "We need to step inside my office."

Then, making eye contact with Todd, he said, "Keep the birds out of my french fries. I'll be back in a few minutes."

Christy and Todd, along with the rest of the lunching tourists, watched as Doug led Katie away from the crowd and under some trees over by the swan-filled moat that surrounded Sleeping Beauty's Castle. He sat down with her on a bench away from the main path of vacationers. With his arms still around her, Doug let Katie cry. She wasn't wailing anymore; at least Christy couldn't hear her.

Christy turned to Todd, aware that people were watching them, and said, "I hope she's okay. Do you think I should go over there?"

"Probably not. She's in good hands with Doug. He has the gift of mercy. That's what she needs right now."

Just then, a small, brown bird hopped up onto the back of

Doug's vacated chair and cocked his head, eyeing Doug's french fries.

"He wasn't kidding about protecting his fries from the birds," Christy said. "Come here, little guy. You leave Doug's fries alone. I'll share mine with you."

She broke off the end of one of her fries and tossed it on the ground near Katie's chair. Immediately the eager bird was joined by his brothers, sisters, aunts, uncles, and cousins, all pecking at the one scrap of french fry.

Christy smiled and began to feed the whole flock. As she did, Todd prayed aloud, with his eyes open, and thanked God for the food and prayed for the Holy Spirit to comfort Katie. Then he added, "I know You care, Father. Your Word says You care about even the smallest bird that falls to the ground, and You provide for all Your living creatures. I know You care about what Katie is feeling. I know You will provide for her emotional needs. Thanks, Papa."

Over the years, Christy had become accustomed to Todd's open way of talking with God. It felt natural and comfortable, even here, out in a patio restaurant in the middle of Disneyland. She felt God's presence, and she felt hopeful that the worst might be over for Katie. She couldn't explain why, but Christy felt strangely comforted and confident that her heavenly Father would always take care of Katie.

Todd and Christy had both finished eating and were tossing their last fries to the birds when Doug and Katie returned. Katie looked red-faced but much more peaceful.

"I'm sorry about that, you guys," she said quietly as she slid back into her chair.

"No need to apologize," Todd said.

"Did you keep the birds out of my fries?" Doug asked.

"It wasn't easy," Christy said. "We had to lure them away with our fries. But it worked."

"Your food is probably cold by now," Katie said sympathetically. "Let me buy you another lunch."

"Since when did a little cooling off stop me from eating anything?" Doug asked, chomping into his big burger. "This tastes fine to me," he garbled through a mouthful of meat.

Katie nibbled at her veggie burger.

Todd asked, "Where to next? You guys think you can handle something a little tamer, like maybe the Jungle Cruise or the Pirates of the Caribbean?"

Doug squinted one eye and in his best pirate accent said, "Me thinks the bloke has Adventureland in his plans."

"We could split up," Christy suggested. "I mean, if you guys don't want to go in the tree house and all that."

"No, I like the tree house," Katie said. "And we have to go to New Orleans Square."

"That's right," said Todd. "I want to get a mint julep and an apple fritter."

"More food?" Doug said. "Count me in!"

It seemed as if nothing had happened. Katie appeared mellow; apparently, releasing the pent-up tears had helped. Doug seemed his happy self and quite unaware that he had single-handedly saved the day.

They finished their lunch without incident, and then Doug turned to Katie and with genuine compassion asked, "If I bought you a Fantasia ice cream cone, would you eat it? Or do you just want a bite of mine?"

"Maybe a bite of yours," Katie said. "I haven't had real ice cream in so long, it might make me sick."

"Wait here, then. I'll be right back. Anyone else want one?"

"I'm too full," Christy said.

"Sure, I'll try anything," Todd said, reaching for the money in his pocket. "How much do you need?"

"My treat." Doug jogged over to the ice cream line. He returned a few minutes later with two huge scoops of what looked like a greenish rocky road ice cream.

"You want the first bite?" Todd said, offering his cone to Christy.

"What? Am I your guinea pig? If I gag on it then you'll know you should accidentally drop it for the birds to clean up?"

"It does look a little weird, doesn't it?" Todd agreed.

"Trust me," Doug said. "It's great stuff. Gourmet. This is the only place you can get it."

"Since when did Doug become a gourmet? He'll eat anything!" Katie said. "Here, let me try it."

Doug held out his cone, and Katie took a dainty bite. Christy and Todd watched.

"That's good," she said. "Let me have another bite. I only got a little bit."

"I'll be glad to get you your own cone, if you want."

"No, just a bite." Katie took another nibble and said, "I'm not kidding, you guys; this is really good!"

Todd and Christy leaned into Todd's cone at the same time and almost bumped noses as they each took a bite. They both leaned back laughing, and at the same time said, "It *is* good!"

"Told you guys," Doug said. Looking at Katie, he asked, "Would you hold this for me for a second?"

Katie took the cone, and Doug popped up and headed for the ice cream window. "Protect that cone from the birds for me, Katie. The only way to do it is to eat the whole thing and don't let a single drop fall to the ground."

"Very tricky," Katie said. "Forcing me back into an addiction to sugar. You should be ashamed of yourself, Doug!"

"Don't get one for me," Christy called out. "I'll share Todd's."

"Oh, you will, huh?" Todd said, taking a big chomp out of the side of the cone.

"This is really good," Katie said. "What are all these little chunks?"

"Cherries," said Todd, taking another bite. "And chocolate chips, I think."

"Wait," Christy said, reaching for her camera. "I have to get a picture of this for the yearbook. Nobody will believe I caught Katie eating ice cream during her senior year. Smile!"

Katie held up the cone and willingly smiled for the camera.

Just then Doug appeared with another cone in each hand.

"I said don't get one for me," Christy said.

"Who said this is for you?" Doug teased.

"What, you think you're going to eat both of those?" Katie asked.

"No, one is for Todd since Christy demolished half of his."

"I did not!"

Doug handed the cone to Todd, and Todd handed the half-eaten one to Christy. "Sounds good to me," Todd said, and he took a man-sized bite out of the new cone.

"Isn't this great stuff?" Katie said. "I love it!" Katie eagerly licked around the bottom of her cone where it was beginning to drip. "This is so good, you guys!"

Doug and Todd looked at each other as if to say, "It's good, but not that good."

"You've been away from sugar for too long," Christy teased. "Welcome back, Katie!"

"You know what?" Katie said with a glimmer of joy returning to her green eyes. "It's good to be back."

CHAPTER SIX

If Only You Knew

"So you really think you would like to live like this?" Doug asked Todd as the four of them crowded into the very top of the Swiss Family Robinson Tree House and surveyed the fake jungle below them.

"Oh, yeah! Can't you just hear the tropical birds and smell the fragrance of the rain-washed leaves on the banana trees?" Todd said.

"Those are mechanical birds with little tape recorders inside their bellies," Katie informed him. "And that's not the scent of rain-washed banana trees. It's the smell of mint julep on Doug's breath. He had three, remember."

"They were small," Doug said. "Besides, Katie, I didn't see you having any trouble putting away your entire apple fritter."

"I know," Katie said with a giggle. "Those were so good!"

Christy was the only one who didn't make fun of Todd's dream to live in the jungle. She saw something wild and wonderful and terrible in his eyes. What was it? The call of God on a man's life? It seemed to Christy that something deep inside was calling to Todd, and he would not rest until he had responded to this mission that for years had whispered to him deep in the night.

"Your turn to pick the next ride, Todd. Jungle Cruise or Pirates?" Katie said.

Todd was leaning over the railing of the tree house, staring at the clumps of scurrying people below. He didn't seem to hear Katie's question.

Christy moved closer to him and put her arm around his shoulder, looking down at whatever it was he was staring at. She tried to imagine what he was thinking. Was he dreaming about jungle life? Sleeping in a hammock? Paddling in his canoe to a neighboring tribe, taking along only his Bible and a spear to catch a fish along the way?

"You know what, Kilikina?"

She loved it when Todd called her by her Hawaiian name. She leaned her head against his shoulder and listened with all her heart.

"There are more lost people in the city than in the jungle today."

Christy pulled back. Where did that come from?

"We're going on down, maties," Doug said in his pirate voice. "We'll be waitin' on ye at the line for the Pirates. Look for us on the starboard side."

"Let's go," Todd said, quickly shaking himself from his daydream and taking Christy by the hand.

She wanted to ask him what he meant by his comment. Was Todd thinking God was calling him to something other than being a missionary in the jungle? After all these years of knowing Todd, she still didn't have him figured out.

Will I ever?

The Pirates of the Caribbean was fun. It reminded Christy of when they had gone on that ride last time and had eaten at the Blue Bayou Restaurant.

When they went on the Jungle Cruise, she noticed that Katie and Doug seemed to be almost cuddled up together. At least they were sitting close. Well, everyone in the boat was, she had to admit. But Doug had his arm across the back of the seat, which made it convenient for Katie to lean up against him. Katie seemed in great spirits. Either she was over her mourning for Michael or she was on a sugar buzz. Or maybe both.

Next they went exploring on Tom Sawyer's Island. Katie seemed to have more fun than the other three put together. They ran across the wobbly bridge, hid in the rock caves, teetered on the balancing rock, and then went on the canoe ride around the island.

Christy took her place in the canoe and held her paddle like an expert. "This is where all my experience from canoeing at summer camp last year is going to pay off," she said.

"But are you sure you can paddle fast without your buns being covered with red ant bites?" Katie said loud enough for everyone on the canoe to hear.

"Doesn't sound like the kind of summer camp I'd like to go to," a large man in front of Christy said over his shoulder.

Christy felt her face turning red and looked down, pretending to adjust her camera.

"Is that getting heavy?" Todd asked. "I can carry it for a while if you want."

"Actually, I should be taking some pictures." Christy took the camera from its case and snapped a couple of shots of Doug and Katie and then two of Todd.

"Here," Doug said, laying his paddle across his lap while everyone else paddled through the water. He reached for the camera. "Let me get one of you and Todd."

Christy leaned against Todd's chest and turned halfway around to face Doug. Todd and Christy smiled. Christy already imagined the kind of frame she was going to buy to put this picture in, a heart-shaped one with flowers around the border.

After the canoe ride, the foursome seemed to be exploring at a slower pace. It was soon dusk, and Todd and Christy left Doug and Katie in the long line for Splash Mountain in order to go retrieve their sweatshirts. They made plans to meet in an hour in Bear Country. Todd and Christy walked hand in hand all the way to the lockers, gathered up the sweatshirts, and headed back down Main Street.

Todd stopped in front of one of the stores and said, "I want to buy something for you."

"You don't have to," Christy said, surprised at Todd's sudden pronouncement.

"I want to. The last time we came here I bought all those things for you with your aunt's money. Ever since then I've wished I had bought something for you with my own money. Something special, just from me to you."

As far as Christy could remember, this was the most tender Todd had ever been. With his arm around her, they browsed through the shop and examined shelves and bins loaded with Disney paraphernalia. Then Christy saw it. It was perfect.

"I'd like this," she said, reaching for the porcelain, heart-shaped frame. It was exactly what she had in mind. "I'm going to put the picture of us in the canoe in this. You know, the picture Doug just took."

"Cool," Todd said. "See anything else you can't live without?"

"Yes," Christy said with a sly grin creeping onto her face, "you."

Todd seemed surprised but honored. "You could live without me, Christy," he answered.

"But I wouldn't want to," she said softly.

Before she knew what was happening, Todd took her face in both his hands, tilted it up, and kissed her. When he drew away, Christy caught her breath and noticed a single tear caught in the corner of his eye. Todd blinked quickly and wrapped his arms around her in a tight hug.

Into her hair he whispered, "Kilikina, if you only knew. If you only knew."

"Knew what?" Christy whispered back. She was aware that people in the crowded store were looking at them, but after Katie's wailing at lunch, this seemed mild.

"Come on," Todd said, letting go and quickly wiping his eyes with the cuff of his blue hooded sweatshirt. "Let's pay for this and then go someplace where we can talk."

Christy slipped her hand into his and followed Todd to the cash register, where he paid for her heart frame. The woman in the ruffled apron carefully wrapped it in tissue, tucked the gift in a bag, and handed it to Christy.

Todd then led Christy down Main Street as if he knew right where he wanted to go to talk. Her curiosity was stampeding through her mind.

What did he mean? If only I knew what?

She didn't like the queasy apprehension bouncing around in her stomach. Was something wrong? Had she done or said something she shouldn't have?

Weaving their way through the crowds in Frontierland, Todd directed Christy toward the big white steamboat docked and ready to take on passengers. The huge Mississippi River replica twinkled with strings of tiny white lights, and on its lower deck a Dixieland jazz band played music to set a person's heart to dancing or at least toes to tapping. Todd didn't seem interested in doing either. He headed up the stairs and made his way over to two empty chairs in the corner of the nearly vacant top deck.

As they sat down, the ship blew its loud whistle and embarked on its journey around Tom Sawyer Island in the coolness of the evening.

"Todd," Christy began, as she faced him, "what's wrong? You're so serious. Was it something I said?"

Todd shook his head and released a puff of a laugh. "No," he said, and then changing his mind, he said, "well, yes, but there was nothing wrong with what you said. It was good. Too good, actually."

"I don't understand. I only said I wouldn't want to have to live without you, and you said if only I knew. Knew what?"

Christy stopped breathing, and all the blood drained from her face. "Todd," she forced the words from her tightening throat, "you're not going to die or something, are you?"

Now Todd really laughed. He tilted his head back and guffawed into the star-filled sky. "No, Kilikina, I'm not going to die. Well, I mean, I am someday. We all are. I don't know when, though, and I don't have any plans to in the near future."

"Then what did you mean?" Christy demanded to know. Her heart was pounding, and she felt flustered. She realized how much she cared for Todd and how much it would hurt if she lost him for any reason.

"I don't know if I can explain it. I want to try, though. Just listen and see if this makes any sense to you."

Christy looked at Todd with wide eyes.

He pressed his lips together and then began slowly. "You know how I'm an only kid and my parents divorced when I was pretty young?"

Christy nodded.

"I sort of grew up by myself and never had anyone to care for or anyone who cared for me. I know my mom and dad both love me, but I would have given anything when I was a kid if they would have decided to love each other again. You know what I mean? It was great that they loved me, but I wanted them to love each other."

Christy thought she saw another tear about to escape from Todd's eye. She squeezed his hand and with her expression urged him to go on. He had rarely talked about his parents, and she wanted him to know he could trust her with the secrets of his heart.

"When I came to know the Lord, it was like God gave me all the love I had missed out on as a kid. It was a secure kind of love. Total acceptance. Grace. God's love changed me. Totally. And I believe God called me to be a missionary. You know, go to the ends of the world and tell people who have never heard about God's love. And it was going to be so easy. I had nothing to give up. No family or anything. And then you came along."

Christy wasn't sure if Todd meant she was interfering with God's plan for his life or what. "Are you saying I'm keeping you from God?"

"No, not at all. You challenge me to grow in my relationship with God. You always have. It's just that you really, truly care about me. You want to be with me. You said in the store you wouldn't want to live without me."

"That's not a bad thing, Todd. I meant it. I care about you more than you can even begin to imagine," Christy said.

"I know," Todd said softly. "You're the first person who ever has."

He didn't say it as if he was trying to feel sorry for himself. It was as if he had made a precious discovery when he realized just how much Christy meant to him.

"That should make you feel good, Todd. Why do you seem bummed out about knowing how much I care?"

The steamboat had completed its circle around the island and was now docked to unload passengers and take on new ones. Todd and Christy remained in their seats, holding hands, locked in their own private world.

"I'm not bummed out. Amazed would be a better word. There's just never been anyone in my life who has cared about me as much as you do. I've pulled away from you in the past, like when I went to Hawaii. Maybe I was afraid of getting too close or caring too much. I don't know." Todd drew in a deep breath as the whistle sounded again, and the ship set out. "I don't know why it's all hitting me so hard or why your words pierced my heart in the store. All I know is that I don't want to live without you either, Kilikina. You are the most precious gift God has ever given to me."

Tears welled up in Christy's eyes, and she felt her lower lip tremble.

Todd stood and moved his chair next to hers so they both faced the front of the boat. He stretched his arm across the back of her chair. Christy nestled her head in the curve of his shoulder and felt his strong jaw resting against her hair.

Without words, they watched the steamboat move into the night as the bright music of the Dixieland band played below them. Above them glittered a thousand night stars, and Christy could hear the steady rhythm of Todd's heart.

Never before had Christy felt so close to Todd and so close to God and so sure that He would keep all of His promises. For perhaps the first time in their relationship, Christy didn't have to wonder if Todd felt the same way she did.

CHAPTER SEVEN

Sunday Best

The shrill sound of the alarm clock roused Christy at 7:30 on Sunday morning. She rolled over, slapped the top of the clock, and let out a groan. "Katie, we have to get up."

"Not yet," Katie mumbled from her rollaway bed on the other side of Bob and Marti's guest room. "Let me sleep five more minutes, okay?"

"I'll hop in the shower first," Christy said, stumbling out of bed. "Church is in an hour."

"I think churches would have much better attendance if they had afternoon services," Katie muttered, pulling the pillow over her head.

"I have a headache," Christy groaned as she stepped into the adjoining guest bathroom. "My feet hurt from walking so much yesterday. I want to go back to bed."

"So go back to bed. We'll meet the guys later this afternoon."

Christy considered hobbling back to bed and diving under the covers, but only for a minute. "No, this is the Lord's day. We need to honor Him and worship with His people."

"I'm worshiping Him in silent praise." Katie's words sounded mushy as she spoke into her pillow.

"I don't think there is such a thing," Christy said, turning on the shower. While waiting for the water to warm up, she examined her face in the mirror. "I look like raw hamburger meat."

"I feel like raw hamburger meat," Katie responded.

"My eyes look like two blowfish caught in a head-on collision," Christy stated, opening her eyes wide and trying to count all the bloodshot lines.

"Christy," Katie said, propping herself up on her elbow and squinting her eyes, "will you and your little blowfish take a shower and let me sleep another five minutes?" She immediately dropped back down on her bed and pulled the covers up over her head.

Giving up any further evaluation of her Disneyland-wearied body, Christy closed the bathroom door, stepped into the shower, and in five minutes was finished. "Your turn," she said brightly to Katie as she opened the door and breezed out in a cloud of steam.

"Already?" Katie groaned, rolling to the edge of her bed in an effort to get up. "Why did we ever say we would go to the first service?"

"I left the shampoo and conditioner in there," Christy said, unwrapping the towel from her wet hair and blotting it dry. "And my curling iron is plugged in on the counter."

"You're acting a little too perky for me, missy," Katie said, plodding her way into the bathroom. "There's nothing worse than watching your best friend fall in love right before your eyes."

"I know," Christy called back as Katie closed the bathroom door. "I did that once, remember?"

For a second she paused, hoping the reference to Michael wouldn't set Katie off emotionally. But then a smile spread across Christy's lips as she slipped into her dress. *Is that what I'm doing?*

Falling in love? Or have I been in love with Todd all along, but neither of us realized it until last night?

She felt like humming. Everything in the world seemed wonderful. Absolutely perfect. It could only get better. In less than an hour she would see Todd. She would slip her hand into his, he would squeeze it tight and hold on to her. They would sit together in church—Todd's church—and sing praises to God. Yes, this morning was definitely a morning to sing.

"Christy?" Bob's voice called out from behind the closed bedroom door and was followed by four gentle taps.

"Yes?"

"Just wanted to make sure you girls were up. I have breakfast ready for you, if you're interested."

"Thanks, Uncle Bob. We'll be down in a few minutes."

"Katie," Christy said, opening the bathroom door and fanning her hand to clear away the steam, "I'm going downstairs. My uncle said he has breakfast ready. Then I'm coming back to do my hair."

"If it's donuts or waffles, save me one."

Christy danced down the stairs. She found Uncle Bob in the kitchen pouring orange juice into tall glasses and placing them next to a platter of fresh cut fruit and assorted muffins and croissants.

"Good morning, Bright Eyes," he said, offering Christy a glass of juice. "How was your day in the Magic Kingdom?"

"Wonderful," Christy said, taking a swig of juice and reaching for a blueberry muffin. "Absolutely wonderful."

"Glad to hear it," Bob said with a smile. "Sounds like a vast improvement over the last time you and Todd went."

"There's no comparison," Christy said. She felt like letting her bursting heart sprinkle its joy all over the kitchen by telling her uncle she was fully in love and had no doubt Todd felt the same way about her.

But just then Aunt Marti walked in. To Christy's surprise, Marti wasn't wearing her Sunday morning robe and slippers. She had donned a becoming blue knit dress, and her hair and make-up were done to perfection. Then Christy noticed that Bob was looking more dressed up than usual.

"You're going to be late," Marti pointed out to Christy. "You can't go to church with your hair still wet."

Christy swallowed her bite of muffin and brushed off her aunt's comment. "Where are you guys going?" she asked.

"With you. To church," Bob said. "It's sort of a favor to Todd. He helped me clean out the garage last week and wouldn't accept any money. Said the only payment he wanted was for us to visit his church. Looks like today is the day."

Christy couldn't believe it. Todd had succeeded in accomplishing what no one else in Christy's family had been able to do. Bob and Marti were going to church.

"I'll dry my hair," Christy said, swallowing another gulp of orange juice and dashing back upstairs.

Katie had just finished drying her hair when Christy entered the room. "Katie, you'll never guess what. Bob and Marti are coming to church with us!"

"That's good," Katie said calmly.

"It's not good," Christy spouted.

"It's not?"

"No, it's better than good. It's unbelievable! It's fantastic. This is a total God thing, Katie. I'm so excited!"

"I can tell," Katie said, scanning Christy's exuberant face. "That's great! Are they ready to go?"

Just then the girls heard the doorbell ring.

"That's probably Todd," Christy said. "I have to hurry!"

Katie stepped away from the sink and let Christy finish getting ready. Katie slipped her shoes on and scrounged in her suitcase for her Bible.

"I'll have to share with you," she called to Christy over the whir of the blow dryer. "I guess I didn't bring my Bible."

"Would you grab mine? It's over on the night stand. And get my purse, too."

"Yes, your majesty. Will there be anything else?"

"Yes, go downstairs and stall for me. Tell them I'll be there in two seconds."

Katie obliged and left Christy with a toothbrush in her mouth, a mascara wand in one hand, and a hot curling iron in the other. "Come on, hair," Christy garbled, her teeth clenching the foaming toothbrush. "Work with me, here. Oh, forget it!" She plopped the curling iron down, gave a few quick swipes of the mascara wand to each eye, and pulled the toothbrush from her mouth, took a quick drink, and swished out her mouth. Then she bent at the waist and tossed all her hair in front of her face, stood up, jerked her head back, and gave her head one more shake. "It's the natural look today," she told her reflection in the mirror and then hurried down the stairs.

Todd stood at the front door waiting for her. The minute they made eye contact, she knew something was different between them. He felt what she felt. For an instant she was sure she was Cinderella, gracefully descending the stairs to meet her Prince Charming.

"Let's go," Marti said briskly, entering the room at top speed. "Is Christy ready yet? Oh, there you are."

As Christy joined Todd, he smiled and took her hand in his. She was delightfully aware that he kept glancing over at her as they hurried down the walkway.

"Is Doug going to meet us there?" Marti asked, letting herself into the front seat of Bob's luxury car.

"Yes," Todd said. "Would you like me to drive my car, too?"

"You three can fit in the back seat," Marti directed.

Katie was already seated next to the far window. Christy slid in next to her, and Todd squeezed in next to Christy.

"Oh, I should have let you sit in front, Todd," Marti said as Bob pulled into the street. "You can sit here on the way home. There's much more room."

Marti chattered all the way to church, apparently wanting to prove she was comfortable in this new experience. Todd's church was big and open. The people were friendly and casual. Many of them wore shorts to church, which seemed to shock Aunt Marti.

Doug had saved a row of seats for them. Marti kept chattering even after the service began, and Christy felt sorry for Katie, who was sitting next to Aunt Marti.

Todd and Doug had no trouble participating in the worship. Christy loved standing between the two of them and hearing their deep, rich voices blend on the praise choruses. She sang her heart out, too. On the last song, Doug and Todd each held one of her hands. Christy was surprised at first, but then she noticed a lot of people were joining hands across the aisles. She peeked over at Bob and Marti. They were holding hands, but neither was singing.

I hope this church isn't too contemporary for them, Christy thought. She noticed that the congregation was a mixture of older and younger people. Plenty of people were Bob and Marti's age. She would love for them to become involved in the church and come to know the Lord personally. It had been her longtime prayer, and now they were actually here, in church, and she didn't want anything to turn them off.

After the singing, everyone sat down, and the pastor took his place on the platform. Instead of standing behind a podium, he perched on a stool and held his open Bible in one hand. His words of teaching were strong, yet compassionate. He spoke with gentle authority. Christy closed her eyes for a moment and pictured Jesus teaching this way, urgently, lovingly coaxing people to turn their lives toward God.

She could imagine Todd being the same kind of teacher as this man. And she could imagine her aunt and uncle responding to the message and giving their hearts to Christ.

During the final portion of the message, the pastor read a verse about how there's no greater love than when a man lays down his life for his friend. He said that was what Jesus did for us, and we show we are truly His disciples when we obey God to the point of giving up that which is most precious to us.

Christy immediately thought of Katie giving up her relationship with Michael because she knew God wanted her to. Christy hoped Katie would be encouraged by this pastor's words and know that she had done the right thing. She also thought the message should be particularly convincing to Bob and Marti.

At the end of the service, the pastor prayed. He said if any individuals wanted to give their lives to the Lord, this was a good time to silently pray, confess their sins, and invite Christ to take over their lives. Christy prayed for Bob and Marti like she had never prayed before.

When they all went out to lunch afterwards, Christy couldn't wait to ask how they liked the service. As soon as they were seated at the large booth, Christy turned to Marti and said, "Did you like the church? Wasn't the message great?"

Marti studied her menu and gave a noncommittal grunt.

"It was different than I expected," Bob said. "He's not the usual black-robed, pulpit-pounding kind of preacher."

"And what kind of church music was that?" Marti asked, peering over the top of her menu and shaking her head. "Guitars and drums! The church I grew up in had an organ. That's proper church music. And that so-called pastor didn't even wear a tie! How does he think people are going to respect his position as a clergyman when he stands up there—or sits up there—looking like one of the original Beach Boys?"

Christy and Todd exchanged glances. Apparently Marti had heard none of the message. She was too distracted by the music and the pastor's appearance. Something inside Christy's heart sank all the way to her big toe. This had been the perfect opportunity for her aunt and uncle to become Christians. But the prospect of either of them making such a decision seemed doubtful. It depressed her. She glanced at her menu but didn't feel hungry for anything now.

"They have a Lighter Fare column here," Marti said, directing Katie to the back of the menu. "I can recommend any of their salads. Be sure to order your dressing on the side, and don't order the house dressing. I understand it's made with sour cream. Terribly fattening."

Katie skipped the Lighter Fare column and stuck with the hamburger column. When the waitress came to take their order, Katie went first. "I'll have the double cheeseburger, fries, and a chocolate shake."

Marti started to laugh. "You have such a fresh sense of humor, Katie, dear."

Katie remained straight-faced.

"She'll have the Hawaiian fruit salad," Marti told the waitress. "And I'll have the same. Dressing on the side for both of us."

"I'm having the cheeseburger," Katie said to the waitress, ignoring Marti's shocked stare. "And could you please add some bacon to that?"

"Katie's come back to the real world," Doug said, leaning across the table and confiding in Bob loudly enough for Marti to hear. "It happened yesterday. I admit, I led her to this destruction with a Fantasia ice cream cone."

"You should be ashamed of yourself," Marti said. She was taking this loss of her health-food comrade seriously. "Do you realize, Doug, it will take her a week to detox from what you let her eat yesterday, and now this—beef and pork and sugar all in one meal!"

Before Marti could rage anymore, the waitress asked, "Would the rest of you like to order, or should I come back?"

"No, we're ready," Bob said. He ordered a patty melt with extra onions. Doug ordered a french dip with a side of onion rings. Todd ordered a turkey sandwich with potato salad, and then it was Christy's turn. She still didn't know what she wanted.

"What is your soup today?" she asked, stalling for time.

"Cream of mushroom and vegetable beef barley."

Both of those gave her the shivers. Now she really didn't know what she wanted, and everyone was waiting for her. Christy hated making decisions; this kind of situation had never been her strength. The worst part was, the only thing that sounded good to her was the Hawaiian salad. But how would it appear if she ordered that after Katie refused it?

"I guess I'll just have the, um . . ." Christy hesitated. *Oh well. What does it matter?* "I'll have the Hawaiian fruit salad."

"Dressing on the side?" the waitress asked.

"Sure. That's fine." Christy closed the menu and handed it to the waitress, fully aware of her aunt's puzzled look.

Christy's choice must have thrown Marti for such a loop that she didn't continue her lecture when the waitress left. Doug jumped right in and began to tell Bob about the highlights of their Disneyland excursion. Katie joined him, and soon a spirited conversation was in full swing around the table.

Todd reached over and grasped Christy's hand under the table. He squeezed it, and she squeezed his back. Instantly, the warm feelings she had experienced at Disneyland returned. An invisible bond seemed to encircle Todd and Christy in their own private bubble. Nothing, Christy was confident, could ever burst it.

CHAPTER EIGHT

Fasten Your Seat Belts, Please

"Good-bye, now," Bob said, patting the side of Christy's car as she and Katie waved at him, ready to drive home after their full weekend.

"Call us when you get home," Marti added. "And drive safely. Do you both have your seat belts on?"

"Yes," Christy called out from her open window. "We're all set. We'll be fine." She slipped the car into gear and eased away from the curb.

"You really don't want to leave yet, do you?" Katie questioned as Christy glanced at her waving aunt and uncle's reflection in the rearview mirror.

"The weekend went too fast," Christy answered with a sigh. "I wish I could have spent some more time with Todd."

"He's coming down to your house next weekend. You can live till then," Katie said.

Christy couldn't tell if Katie was teasing or being sarcastic. Katie seemed to have made considerable progress in recovering from the loss of Michael after her emotional release at Disneyland. Still, Christy couldn't help but wonder if a few more tears weren't left inside Katie. Christy decided to redirect the conversation.

"There are some CD's in a box under the seat. Do you want to find us some traveling music?"

Katie reached for the box. "What do you want to listen to?" Then, before she lifted the lid, Katie said, "Oh, wait! I have a new CD in my backpack. Doug gave it to me."

"Doug gave it to you?"

"Yeah, this morning in the parking lot after church. He said it had some songs he really liked, and he thought I might like them, too. Wasn't that nice of him?" Katie unlatched her seat belt and knelt on the front seat, reaching into the luggage in the back.

"Careful," Christy said, checking her rearview mirror, which was filled with the reflection of Katie's backside. "Try to hurry, okay?"

It was dusk. Christy turned on her lights and gingerly merged into the traffic on Pacific Coast Highway.

"Where is that thing?" Katie leaned farther into the backseat.

Christy wanted to say to Katie, as if she were a child, "Sit back down right this instant! Do you realize how dangerous that is?" But instead she nibbled on her lower lip and checked her side mirror. To her horror she saw blue flashing lights.

"Katie . . . is that a policeman behind us?"

Katie popped her head up, checked the car behind them, and with a friendly wave said, "Yep, looks like he's trying to get your attention. Hey, Mr. Policeman!"

Just then the siren went on, and Christy felt her heart stop. "What do I do? What do I do?" she sputtered.

Katie twisted around and plopped back in her seat. "Relax! You didn't do anything wrong. Pull over to the right. Where's your registration? In here?" She opened the glove compartment and began to shuffle through the papers as Christy nervously pulled the car over to the side of the road and rolled down her window before turning off the engine.

"Now what do I do?"

"Wait and be cool. He'll come to you."

"Should I get out my license? Where's my purse?"

"Relax! It's right here," Katie said, handing Christy her purse. "And here's Mr. Policeman."

Christy turned to face a stern-looking man who leaned on the window rim and peered in the car, taking a good look at Katie.

"Good evening, officer," Katie said with a smile.

The policeman then looked at Christy and said, "May I see your license and registration, please?"

"It's right here," Christy handed him her whole wallet.

"All I need is your license," he said. "Would you mind taking it out?"

"Oh, sure. Sorry." Christy fumbled with her wallet while Katie thumbed through a small stack of papers she had pulled from the glove compartment.

"Here's the registration," Katie said, holding out the paper to the officer before Christy had managed to pull her license out of her wallet.

The officer waited.

"I almost have it," Christy said with a nervous laugh. Her hands were shaking so badly she could barely get a grip on the slick piece of paper. "There." She handed it to the officer. He looked the papers over and then pulled a pad of paper out of his back pocket.

Just then a garbled message came over his car radio. He said something about staying put and walked back to his car. Christy closed her eyes and let out a heavy sigh.

"Why are you so stressed?" Katie said. "You probably have a taillight out or something. It's nothing. Relax."

When Christy opened her eyes, she was aware of all the cars zooming past them. She felt certain all those people were laughing at her, snickering at her embarrassment. This was awful.

"Okay, Miss Miller," the officer said, striding up to her car. "You lucked out. I have to respond to this call right away." He handed her papers back and quickly looked into the car, making eye contact with Katie. "I suggest you put your seat belt on and keep it on. The next officer might not be in such a hurry." He rushed back to the patrol car, turned on the lights and siren, and pulled out into the traffic.

Still quivering, Christy crammed the papers and wallet into her purse and turned the car on.

"What was that supposed to mean?" Katie said.

"You didn't have your seat belt on," Christy said sharply. "I almost got a ticket because you didn't have a seat belt on."

"It was only for a minute. I was going to put it back on after I found the CD."

Christy took her time pulling back into the traffic flow.

"Are you sure that's what the problem was?" Katie asked defensively.

"Yes."

"Well, then why didn't you tell me there was a policeman behind us? I wouldn't have been so obvious about retrieving the stuff in the backseat."

"It doesn't matter if a policeman is there or not. You're supposed to keep your seat belt on," Christy snapped back.

"Okay, okay, it's on." She clicked it hard for added emphasis. "Man, you would think you actually got a ticket the way you're acting!"

"But I could have."

"But you didn't!"

"But I almost did!"

"But," Katie spoke each word firmly, "you didn't."

Several minutes passed before Christy broke the stubborn silence. "I'm sorry, Katie. I was nervous. It really freaked me out."

"No, it's my fault," Katie said. "You're right. Just because we didn't suffer a consequence this time doesn't mean I did the right thing by taking off my seat belt. Like the guy said, we lucked out. Or should we say it was a God thing?"

Christy shot a smile at Katie. It was nice to hear Katie use her old favorite phrase and call something a God thing. It was good to have Katie back.

"Pull in there," Katie said, pointing to a convenience store on the right side of the road.

Christy made the turn and parked in front of the brightly lit store. "Good idea. I should call my parents and tell them where we are."

"I need something to drink. How about you?" Katie asked.

"Sure. I could go for some juice."

"I'll get it for you," Katie said, pushing open the store's door and greeting the clerk with a friendly hello as if she knew him.

Christy dialed her home. She decided to save the part about being stopped by a policeman until she got home, and only told her mom they were just past Laguna Beach. Mom gave all the usual instructions about being careful, and Christy said, "Don't worry, Mom. We will."

"Ready?" Katie asked, exiting the store with a bottle of orange juice in one hand and a bag in the other.

Christy nodded and unlocked Katie's door. They crawled in, and as Christy started up the car, Katie said, "I picked up a few supplies for the rest of the journey home. Are you ready for a Twinkie?"

"A Twinkie? Do you know how long it's been since I've seen you with a Twinkie in your hand?"

"Yes," Katie said, tearing off the clear wrapper and sinking her teeth into the yellow sponge cake. "Too long." There was a dot of white frosting on her top lip.

Christy laughed. "It's nice having you back, Katie. I'll take one of those Twinkies, if you have enough."

"Enough?" Katie said, opening the grocery bag and holding it up so Christy could see inside. At least eight packages of a variety of non-Michael-approved junk food lurked inside.

Katie handed Christy an opened Twinkie. She then pulled out a bag of chips for herself. "Let's hope my next boyfriend, if there ever is one, is a connoisseur of the finer things in life. Like Doritos. Ranch flavored." With that she chomped down on the chip in her mouth.

"Are you going to be okay seeing Michael tomorrow?" Christy asked cautiously. "I mean, he's in your government class, right?"

"I'll be okay. I think. I don't know. I don't want to think about it. I don't trust any of my emotions at this point. I wanted to tell you, though, that being with you guys this weekend really helped. I had a great time. Doug went above and beyond the call of duty in helping me feel better. He's a great guy. I think he should be a counselor."

"Well, if it gets rough this week, I'm here for you."

"Thanks, Christy." Katie snapped another chip and said, "Do you know what's weird? I feel that while I was with Michael I was in a time warp. I'm outside of it now, so I feel normal. But when I was with him, being in his world seemed normal. Does that make sense?"

"Sort of."

"The thing is, I don't think I did anything wrong. I mean, I know I didn't do anything wrong morally. Michael's standards were just as high as mine. That wasn't really a problem. Who knows? It might have been a problem eventually, if we had gone together longer. You want some chips?"

"No, thanks." Christy licked the last Twinkie crumbs from her lips and urged Katie to keep talking while she kept her eyes on the road.

"Do you think it's possible that it was really God's will I go out with him just to tell him about the Lord, even though Michael didn't make a commitment to Christ? At least now he's heard. Maybe I was the only one God could use to tell him."

"Maybe," Christy said cautiously.

"And maybe he'll become a Christian soon, and we'll get back together." Katie turned in her seat to face Christy and wiggled to get comfortable in her seat belt. "Maybe the whole reason we broke up was to force him to look at the Lord without me there to bug him about it."

"Maybe," Christy said.

"I don't know," Katie said. "I don't know what I think. All I know is when I first started going out with him I knew somewhere deep inside my heart that it wasn't right. But I didn't think we would be together for very long, and I knew I wasn't going to do anything wrong. What would it hurt? Then one date turned into two, and then three and, well, you know the rest."

Katie crumpled up the empty bag of chips and tossed it in the sack, rummaging around for a bag of candy. "So my question is, did I do anything wrong by dating a guy who's not a Christian? Everyone always tells us not to, but sometimes it's okay, isn't it? Like when it's just a short time, and nobody gets really hurt. I mean, I came out of this whole relationship fine. Sure, I still hurt a little, but I think I'm going to be okay. I'm a better person. I obeyed God when He told me to break up. It was okay this one time, wasn't it?"

Christy had strong opinions about only dating Christians, and she and Katie had talked about it before. Of course, as Katie had pointed out, it was easy for Christy to say that when she was dating Todd. But it was a lot harder to say those same things when no decent Christian guys were around.

"I think the guideline exists for a reason," Christy said.

"Right, I know. So you won't marry a non-believer and end up 'unequally yoked.' But don't you think it's okay if it's for a short time and nobody gets hurt? Just a friendship. Don't you think that stuff about not dating unbelievers is totally, grossly overemphasized?"

Christy tried to think of a way to tell Katie what she thought yet somehow tone it down so it didn't come out as intensely as she felt it. Suddenly a peculiar analogy came to her. "Actually, Katie, I guess with Michael you lucked out. It would have been different if the officer didn't have another call or if we'd actually gotten in an accident."

"What are you talking about? Are we having the same conversation here?"

"You know, all that talk about wearing your seat belt is grossly overemphasized. You're not planning to get in an accident. You guys only went out for a little while. Still, I'd say you lucked out."

"Are you talking about my dating Michael or my taking off my seat belt?"

"Both."

Katie let the full meaning of the analogy sink in. "Oh" was all she said.

Christy immediately felt bad. "I'm sorry, Katie. I shouldn't have said that. That was judgmental of me. You're right, I was too self-righteous and judgmental the whole time you were dating, and that wasn't right."

"No, you don't have to apologize. I deserve all your words and more. I live too much on the edge. I take off my seat belt and think it's okay as long as I don't get caught. I become involved emotionally with a guy who's not a Christian and think it's okay just because we're not going beyond my standards." Katie took a deep breath. She rested her bag of M&M's on her lap. "But you're right, Christy. There's a higher level of accountability that's not based on whether or not you get caught."

Katie crumpled the candy bag and stuffed it back in the sack. Sitting up straight, she made a declaration. "Hear ye, hear ye. From this day forward, the new, improved Katie is going to strive for integrity in all things. Even in what I eat. That's probably the best thing that came out of my relationship with Michael, an appreciation for healthy food. I'm going to go back to eating right. And I'm going to keep exercising regularly and start reading my Bible every day, and I am not going to gossip ever again."

They were now approaching the interchange with the freeway that would take them back to Escondido. Christy signaled in plenty of time, got in the right lane, and followed the curve in the road up, over and onto Interstate 78. She needed to concentrate on changing lanes, so she held back from responding to Katie until they were securely in the middle lane.

"You're a good influence on me," Katie said. "You do everything right."

"No, I don't."

"Yes, you do. You're much more conscientious than I am. Much more concerned about doing the right thing."

"I don't do the right thing any more often than you do."

"Oh, yes you do. You have a certain quality. Anyone can see it by just looking at your face. You're without guile, Christy."

"Whatever that means. It sounds like a curse," Christy said with a laugh.

"Not at all." Katie shook her head. "I'd say it's a blessing. Just look at your life. Everything is perfect. You've never hit a wall with God. I mean, what's the worst thing that could ever happen to you?"

"I don't know. I guess my parents could die."

"Then you'd go live with Bob and Marti and be pampered to death. And the only other awful thing would be if Todd broke up with you."

There was a moment of jaw-clenching silence.

Then Katie said, "But that would never happen. Don't you see? You are living with the reward of having your relationships according to God's way and in His time. I want that kind of blessing on my life, too."

Christy wasn't sure it all worked as neatly as Katie claimed.

CHAPTER NINE

Sweet Dreams

It was the fastest week on record, Christy was sure. She couldn't believe it was Friday already. She was driving to the pet store after school, but she wished she was going home instead. She could use a nap.

Every night that week Christy had stayed up until after eleven, studying. The worst part was, everyone said it would be like this for another three weeks until finals. She didn't think she could keep up the pace. But she had no choice. What kept her going was knowing Todd would come up tomorrow.

"Wonderful," Christy spoke into the stillness of the car. "No, marvelous. No, no, no. Delicious. Fantastic. Unbelievably terrific!"

No, that's still not it, she insisted. How can I describe what I'm feeling? How do I put my thoughts about Todd into words? It's too good to be true. This must be love. But how do I describe it?

As Christy parked her car and took quick steps into the mall, she realized her problem was a common one. What was it her English teacher had said last year? Through all the generations, poets, composers, and artists have tried to describe love. Yet no one has completely captured it, so the world is still full of poets, composers, and artists who continue in the footsteps of their fore-fathers, attempting to portray love, yet never with complete success.

"Hi, Jon," Christy said, taking her position behind the cash register.

"Hi. I've been meaning to ask you how your bunny is."

Christy thought Jon said "honey." It seemed strange that he would ask about Todd that way.

"He's fine. I'm going to see him tomorrow."

Jon gave her a puzzled look and said, "Has he been eating well?"

Christy laughed. "Of course. He eats all the time. Why do you ask?"

"No reason. It's just that if they're not feeling well, they tend to stop eating. What about spending time with him? You still hold him a lot, don't you? Give him lots of snuggles and love?"

Now Christy really laughed, only it was an embarrassed laugh. She glanced around to make sure no customers in the store could hear their conversation.

"Yes, I give him lots of snuggles. Why in the world are you asking?"

"Because I know how easy it is to end up neglecting the little guy when you're not around him all the time."

"The little guy?"

"Don't your parents make you keep him in the garage?"

"In the garage?" Christy questioned.

"Isn't that where Hershey's cage is? In the garage? You know, Hershey, the rabbit I gave you a couple of months ago."

"Oh, Hershey! Yes, his cage is in the garage." Christy tried to stifle her laughter.

"Why? Who did you think I was talking about?" Jon asked.

"Never mind," Christy said, grateful and relieved that a customer had stepped in front of Jon and placed an aquarium filter on the counter.

Christy smiled at the woman and said, "How are you today?"

"Fine, thanks. Is this one on sale?"

"Yes," Christy said, double-checking the price sticker. "This one is twenty percent off."

"Yeah, well, it's not the only one," Jon said loud enough for Christy to hear.

She shot him a quick glance and then focused back on the customer. "That's fifteen cents change for you." Christy placed a dime and a nickel in the woman's open palm and, handing her the bag, said, "Thanks a lot. Have a nice afternoon."

The woman smiled and left. Another customer stepped up to the counter. Christy went through the process of scanning the merchandise, ringing it up on the cash register, and making change. She had done this so many times she could almost do it in her sleep, which was a good thing. She was incredibly tired. She had a hard time staying alert until closing at nine.

"You look as if you're all ready to go," Jon commented as Christy began to pull down the metal cage door that closed the pet store off from the rest of the mall. "We still have two more minutes."

"Do you want me to put the door back up?"

"No, that's fine. You go ahead and leave. You look beat. I'll close up."

"Preparing for finals," Christy offered by way of explanation. "Get used to this walking-in-my-sleep look. I'll probably be like this for the next few weeks."

"Do you want to take some time off? I have a new guy starting next Wednesday, and he was asking for more hours than I could give him. It would just be until you want the hours back," Jon said.

"I'd miss the money, but it would sure help right now." Christy thought a moment and then said, "You know, if it would be okay, I could use the next few weekends off. Maybe the next three?" In the back of her mind she was trying to calculate when the prom was. She wanted to be prepared in case she and Todd decided to go. It was almost too late to buy tickets, but she wanted to leave every door open.

"Okay," Jon said, reaching for the clipboard behind the register. "Let's say you work tomorrow and then again on Friday a month from now. Is that too much time off?"

"It sounds like a lot."

"It's up to you."

"I think it's fine. Go ahead and give the other guy my hours. I need to make it through this next intense month of school. Thanks for being so understanding, Jon."

"It's part of my managerial role. Besides, who says I'm too old to remember how stressful the end of your senior year can be? You take it easy. And try to get some sleep, okay?"

"I will. Thanks, Jon. See you tomorrow morning."

Christy barely remembered her head hitting the pillow that night. On Saturday morning her mom came in to wake her up at 10:15.

"Christy? Time to get up, honey. You need to leave for work in half an hour."

"Ohhhh," Christy groaned. "My head is pounding."

"Are you feeling all right?"

"My throat is swollen. I feel awful!"

Mom placed her cool hand on Christy's cheek. "Feels like you're running a temperature. When did this start?"

"I was tired yesterday." Christy swallowed. It felt as if she had a wad of gum stuck in her throat. "My throat didn't hurt, though. And I didn't ache this much, either."

"I think you'd better stay in bed. Do you want me to call work for you?"

"I guess," Christy groaned. "Tell Jon I'm going to sleep some more, and if I feel better, I'll work this afternoon."

Mom left the room, and Christy rolled over and kicked off her sheets. She felt as though she was burning up. She could hear her pulse pounding in her inner ear.

What happened to me? I feel awful.

"Okay," Mom said a few minutes later, entering Christy's room. "Jon said he doesn't want you to come in at all. He has someone to cover your hours, and he didn't want you to bring any flu bugs into work."

"Thanks, Mom."

"Jon also told me about your arrangement to take time off for the next few weeks. I think that was wise of you. Perhaps you should have started sooner. Do you feel like taking a bath? That would be the best thing for the aches."

"I guess," Christy said feebly. Ever since she was a child she was used to special treatment when she got sick. Her mom seemed like a natural nurse, bringing Christy juice, taking her temperature, and scanning the vitamin book to find a natural cure for every ailment. It was easy for Christy to surrender to her mom's babying.

"I'll go run the water in the tub."

Christy slowly sat up in bed. The room felt as if it were spinning. Today reminded her of one of her greatest fears: One day she would be mature and self-sufficient, living in a college dorm room or an apartment. She would come down with some kind of killer flu, and she wouldn't have her mom to take care of her.

Standing on wobbly feet and inching her way across the carpeted floor, Christy shuffled to the bathroom, where Mom had already placed a tray with ice water in a glass with a straw, several vitamins, and two aspirins on a napkin. Christy noticed an unpleasant fragrance rising from the steaming tub.

"I've put some apple cider vinegar in the water," Mom said. "The book said it helps to draw out the toxins. Soak in there for at least twenty minutes, okay?"

"You're starting to sound like Katie," Christy said, realizing that it hurt her throat to talk. She twisted her hair up on top of her head and secured it with a clip.

"I'm going to change the sheets on your bed and air your room out." Mom closed the bathroom door. Christy could hear her humming as she went about her nursing tasks.

Gingerly lowering herself into the stinky, steaming water, Christy closed her eyes and imagined what it would be like to get sick if she were Katie's roommate. She could picture Katie popping her head into Christy's room and saying, "Oh, you're sick? Well, don't worry about answering the phone. I'll put the machine on. There's some leftover Chinese take-out from a couple of days ago. I won't be back until late tonight, so don't bother to wait up for me."

Yes, the image of independent life made her grateful still to be at home and to have her mom to take care of her. Even the water didn't smell so bad, once she snuggled all the way in and grew used to it.

She soaked until the water felt cool and her fingers felt wrinkly. But when she stood up, she didn't feel much better. Only dizzy. Mom had delivered a clean set of sweats to the bathroom, which Christy put on. Even her feet hurt as they plunged into the legs of the sweatpants.

Glancing in the mirror, Christy thought, *Scary! Look at the dark rings under my eyes. I'm glad Todd isn't here to see me looking like this.*

Then it hit her. Todd was coming today!

"Mom!" Christy called out hoarsely, opening the bathroom door and making her way back to her bed by the most direct route possible. She found her room looking fresh and her sheets changed with the corner of the covers turned down, inviting her to crawl in. Even the clutter on her floor had been picked up. On her nightstand stood another glass of ice water with a bent straw and a box of throat lozenges. Christy slid in between the sheets and felt as if a million pounds had been lifted from her when her head touched the soft pillow.

"How are you feeling?" Mom said, entering the room carrying a tray adorned with a cup of tea and some dry toast. "You want to try to eat something?"

Christy shook her head. "Todd," she whispered, trying not to strain her sore throat. "Call him and tell him not to come."

"Oh, dear," Mom said. "I hope he hasn't left yet. I'll call him right away."

Christy felt exhausted from the hot bath. Her bed was clean and comforting, and her room smelled fresh. The fragrance from Mom's can of Lysol was a vast improvement over the apple cider vinegar bath. Christy sniffed, thinking she could still smell some of the vinegar. Then she fell asleep.

Sometime later, she felt a cool hand on her forehead. Without opening her eyes, she whispered, "Todd?" as a question to see if Mom had called him.

"I'm right here," Todd's deep voice answered. He removed his hand from her forehead and took her hand in his. "How are you doing?"

"I . . . but, you . . ." She tried to express that she was sorry he had come all this way when she was sick. But the words were caught in her swollen throat, and she swallowed them.

"Hey, don't try to talk. You should drink something, though. Here, let me hold this for you." Todd lifted the glass of ice water to her lips, and she obediently sipped from the straw. The coldness felt good on her raw throat, and she drank nearly half the glass before letting go of the straw.

"Good job. We'll do that again in about five minutes. Your mom gave me strict orders to make you drink water and take all your pills. Think you can manage this one?" He placed a small vitamin between her lips and held the glass of water for her. She swallowed the pill, even though it hurt going down, and drank most of the rest of the glass of water.

"Want some more water?"

Christy shook her head.

"Go back to sleep. I'll be here," Todd said. "I have some reading to do. You have some recuperating to do."

"I'm sorry," Christy forced out the words.

"Sorry for what? Sorry you're sick? I'm sorry you're sick, too. That doesn't change anything. I wanted to spend some time with you, and that's what I'm doing. You rest. Don't worry about me. I have finals to study for, and there's no place I'd rather sit and study than by your side."

As Christy slipped off into a dream, she thought of how those were probably the sweetest words Todd had ever said to her. No, the sweetest words anyone had ever said to her. Even though she still felt sick, her heart soared.

It was late afternoon when Christy began to wake up. She

remembered the feel of Todd's hand on her forehead and thought it must have been part of her dream.

He had placed his hand on her forehead like that once before. It was early morning on the beach a year and a half ago. Todd was about to leave for Hawaii, and Christy had begun to date a guy named Rick. As Todd's farewell, he had placed his cool hand on Christy's forehead and blessed her, saying, "The Lord bless you and keep you. The Lord make His face to shine upon you and give you His peace. And may you always love Jesus first, above all else."

Surely Todd's hand on her forehead had been just a memory evoked by her feverish dreams. She now had only to open her eyes to verify if it was a dream. She hesitated. Keeping her eyes closed, she decided it would be better to continue in her lovely dream than to see nothing but thin air beside her bed.

But the sound of someone moving in a chair prompted her to open her eyes. And there he was. For real. A dream come true. Todd's blond head was bent over a thick textbook, a notebook was draped on his lap, and a pencil was in his mouth. Christy tried to lie as still as she could, watching Todd without his knowing she was awake.

That's when she realized her throat didn't feel quite so swollen anymore, and her head wasn't throbbing, either. She actually felt a lot better.

Just then her bedroom door squeaked open, and Christy snapped her eyes shut and pretended to be asleep.

She heard her mom's voice whisper, "How's our patient?"

Footsteps followed closer to the bed.

"Still sleeping," Todd answered. "Her fever seems to be down."

"Good," Mom whispered back. "You know, Todd, this is

above and beyond the call of friendship to spend your whole day here with her."

"I'm getting a lot done," Todd said and then added with a hint of teasing in his voice, "since it's quieter here than in the library. Besides," now his voice turned serious, "what I feel for Christy is above and beyond the call of friendship."

Christy couldn't believe Todd said that to her mom. Her heart began to beat a little faster. It was one thing for Todd to reveal his feelings to Christy at Disneyland, but it was quite another to say something to her mother. She never would have imagined such a moment.

"You know you have our blessing in that area," a deep voice said.

My dad is in here, too? Todd said that in front of Dad, and he said Todd has his blessing? This has to be a dream!

Christy stretched her long legs beneath the covers and pretended to be stirring from her sleep. With the finesse of an actress, she let out a slight sigh and fluttered her eyes open.

Her dad and mom were standing beside her bed, and Todd was still seated at the foot. As soon as she opened her eyes, Todd leaned forward and reached for her hand, giving it a squeeze.

"Well, Sleeping Beauty, did you have sweet dreams?"

She felt like telling him the conversation she awoke to was sweeter than any dream ever. Their eyes met, and she wondered if Todd knew she had overheard their conversation.

"Your fever seems to be gone," Mom said, feeling Christy's forehead. "You look better around the eyes. How's your throat?"

"It's lots better."

"Good! Now you should eat some soup. I'll get it."

Christy's dad brushed his large, gruff hand across her flushed cheek. "Glad you're feeling better."

"Thanks, Dad." Christy smiled at him. She was amazed that she could be in bed, holding hands with her boyfriend while exchanging tender, meaningful smiles with her dad. It all seemed natural. Sweet. In every way, a dream come true.

CHAPTER TEN

Weird and Tweaked

"You're here!" Katie said, coming up behind Christy at her locker on Monday morning. "I called this weekend, and your mom said you were sick. Are you better?"

Christy closed her locker, and the two of them maneuvered their way through the crowded hallway. "I'm getting there. I might go home after lunch, but I didn't want to get behind in my classes. I have something to tell you at lunch, though. Can you meet me out at the tree?"

"Sure. And I have something to tell you that you won't believe!" Katie's eyes sparkled as she waved and called out, "Ta-ta!" before ducking into her classroom.

I wonder what's up? Does it have something to do with Michael?

It was torture sitting through her classes, waiting for lunch so she could find out what Katie's secret was. Finally the lunch bell rang, and Christy hurried out to their meeting spot.

"You go first," Katie said, sitting on the ground beneath the tree where they usually ate. It was also the spot where Katie had first met Michael at the beginning of the school year.

"No, you go. My curiosity is overflowing."

"It's about Fred," Katie said excitedly.

"Oh," Christy retorted flatly. "Maybe I should go first. My news about Todd is definitely more exciting than anything you could tell me about Fred."

"Not necessarily," Katie said coyly.

"Okay, go ahead. What about Fred?"

"He came to church yesterday," Katie said. "He sat next to me."

Christy wasn't impressed. She bit into her apple and said, "He asked about church. I told you that, didn't I? I'm glad he went. Now, do you want to hear about Todd?"

"I have more," Katie said. "After church we walked out to the parking lot together. When we got to my car, Fred said, 'So, how do I give my heart to God, like that minister talked about?'"

Christy lost interest in her apple. "Really? That's great! What did you tell him?"

Katie looked as if she were about to bubble over with excitement. "I just told him that God knew his heart. If he wanted to get things right between him and God, all he had to do was ask God to forgive him for everything wrong he had ever done and then invite the Lord to take over his life."

"And?" Christy said.

"And he and I prayed right there in the parking lot by my car. Fred gave his heart to the Lord."

"I don't believe it."

"I know. What a God thing! It was so incredible. He was so ready, I felt as if I just stood there and watched. All these months of trying to convince Michael to give his life to God. All our long conversations, and all my explanations and pleadings, and here Fred, of all people, follows me to my car and gets saved!"

Christy laughed with joy. "That's great! It was kind of the same way with Alissa. I mean, Todd and I had been praying for her, but then one afternoon on the beach she said 'I'm ready,' and her life has never been the same since."

"I don't understand why it was so easy for Fred and impossible for Michael," Katie commented, opening her sack and looking inside.

"Who knows. God is weird," Christy said reverently. "Not weird like goofy, but weird like unexplainable."

"Yeah, God is weird, and we are tweaked," Katie surmised. "That's my philosophy of life. God's way of doing things is never our way, and we're bent. Tweaked. We always want to do things in a way that's twisted from God's."

"I like that," Christy said. "Only you could put it so eloquently."

"So when you see Fred in yearbook next period, act real excited for him."

"Don't worry! I won't have to act; I *will* be!"

True to her word, Christy was excited for Fred when she told him, "I'm so glad you've become a Christian! That's the best thing that could ever happen to you, Fred."

Fred beamed his toothy smile and said, "And the second best thing would be if you went to the prom with me. I already have the tickets, you know."

Christy's enthusiasm stopped cold. Is that why Fred started going to church and said he became a Christian? Was it all part of a scheme to become involved in Christy's world? And how could she ask him without sounding accusatory?

"Fred," she began, "I am not going to the prom with you. Not even because you've become a Christian."

Fred's face fell. "You think that's why I did it?"

"Well, no. I just want you to know I really can't go with you. I have a boyfriend. If I do go, it will be with him."

Fred turned and walked away. Was he hurt? Mad? Finally giving up? She wondered if she should follow him to the other side of the classroom. But then, what would she say?

Instead, she slipped into her desk and breathed out a heavy sigh. *At least now Fred knows I won't go out with him. I'm sorry to hurt his feelings, but his bugging me about the prom has gone far enough. He'll be okay. He'll bounce back. He always does.*

She and Todd needed to decide tonight if they were going to the prom. That would settle the matter once and for all. She tried to concentrate on her reading, knowing this free class time would enable her to lessen her homework load. But all she could think about was Todd.

He had been wonderful to stay with her all day Saturday. Then he had called and talked to her for almost two hours on Sunday. Their conversation had been full of plans for the upcoming weeks and even into the summer. Christy hadn't brought up the prom, though, and she didn't know if Todd was even interested.

She called him that night and started out by asking what he thought about the prom.

"It's a poor imitation of the real thing."

"What?" Christy asked, not following him.

"It's like pretending you're at the wedding feast. It's a poor imitation of the real thing."

"You mean, you think people who go to the prom are pretending like they're getting married?" It had a certain ring of truth, Christy thought. She had heard from some of the girls how much they were spending on their dresses. Then there was the whole extravaganza of flowers, tux, and the limo.

"You see, I think that what every human soul longs for, whether that person knows it or not, is to be at the marriage feast of the Lamb," Todd explained.

"You lost me," Christy said.

"Christy. You know, when this world comes to an end and we all stand before God, He's going to bring all those whom He's prepared to be the Bride of Christ—the Church—into the marriage feast, where the Believers and Christ will be united forever. It's going to be the biggest, wildest party ever."

Christy guessed Todd must be talking about prophecies from the Bible, from the book of Revelation. It was an area she didn't know a lot about.

"So deep within the heart of every person is the desire to be invited," Todd continued, "to be dressed like royalty and treated the same, and to be included in the celebration. Something like a prom is a hollow imitation of the real thing you and I will experience one day."

Now Christy felt annoyed. It was one thing to have an opinion about the prom. It was another thing to have the blessed hope to spend eternity celebrating around God's throne. But to overlap these two and invalidate the prom in light of heaven was ridiculous.

"Todd, I know you like to see something spiritual in everything, and I think that's great. But this is just the prom. It's a human, earthly celebration, and I don't see how it has anything to do with heaven. May I rephrase my original question? Would you like to go to the prom with me?"

"If you really want to go."

Christy hated answers like that. It wasn't an answer; it only put the question back on her. "I don't know what I want. That's why I'm asking what you want."

"Let's talk about it, then," Todd said. "How much does it cost? Do we want to go with some others or by ourselves? Do you want to go out to dinner first? Do you have a dress or money to buy a dress? And most importantly, why do you want to go?"

For twenty minutes the two of them tossed back and forth the pros and cons. In the end, Christy said, "I don't know. I still feel as if I could go either way. It would be fun and wonderful and romantic to get all dressed up and go with you, but it would take all our money, and I'm not into dancing."

"It's up to you," Todd said, putting the decision back in her lap again. "If we do go, you need to know that even if you don't see a parallel between the two, while I'm at the prom I'm going to be thinking about heaven and our ultimate celebration there one day."

After Christy hung up, she wasn't sure how to take Todd's comments. Did he mean that he wouldn't be focusing on her that evening or admiring her or enjoying being with her because he would be centering his thoughts on eternal things? Why did Todd have to be like that? God was always first in his life.

Then Christy realized that was a compliment, not a slam. It was a rare thing to be so focused on God. Todd seemed to see God's perspective on everything.

Christy decided to let go of the prom question and focus on her homework so she could get some sleep. Her flu bug had passed, but she felt weak and ready for bed at 5:30. She decided to put all her energies into studying this week. When she saw Todd over the weekend, they could come to a conclusion about the prom. That would still give them two weeks to make any arrangements. She could come up with a dress by then—couldn't she?

Even though she thought she had set the prom question aside for the week, it kept popping up in her mind. After all, she would remind herself, this was her senior year. She was graduating. She had a boyfriend. It was only natural they should go to the prom. Secretly, she would love to show off Todd to all the other girls in her class. More than that, though, she would love to have a reason to dress up and be with Todd in a formal setting. He was always so casual. She had only seen him dressed up a few times, and she had never danced with him.

Not that Christy was sure she knew how to dance. She had never been to a dance and had never really learned how to dance.

The more she thought about it, the more complicated the whole thing became. She had almost $450 saved up from work, and it killed her to think that if she did go to the prom, it would cut deeply into her savings. And Todd didn't have much money. How much was she expecting him to pay for the tux, flowers, dinner, and the tickets?

The more she thought about it, the more frustrated she became. Two years ago, Rick had asked her to his prom, and her parents had said absolutely not. She was a sophomore then. Now she was a senior. Her parents hadn't been fond of Rick. They liked Todd. Still, what would they say if she told them she wanted to go?

CHAPTER ELEVEN

I'll Be Here

"Are you sure you don't want to come to Newport Beach with me this weekend?" Christy asked Katie over the phone on Thursday night. "We had such a good time a couple of weeks ago. I have the weekend off work, and I'm taking my books to study with Todd. You know you're welcome to come."

"I know, but I feel like staying home. Can you believe I just said that?" Katie said. "I feel I need time to sort things out. I talked to Michael yesterday."

"Was that the first time?"

"Yeah. It was awful. He's such a sweetheart. I love him. I truly do. Do you think it's possible to genuinely love someone even though that's not the person you'll marry?"

Christy gave it some thought. "I think it is possible, Katie."

"Do you suppose that for the rest of your life in some small way you remain in love with him?"

"Maybe. I don't know. That would sure hurt for a long time if you did. Maybe you grow out of love the more you're away from that person. You then grow in love with someone else, and it dims the memory of that first love."

"Do you really think so?"

"I don't know."

"Well, if I am going to grow out of love with Michael, all I know is that it's going to take longer than two weeks."

"Are you sure you want to stay home this weekend? It seems like you'll be depressed the whole time."

"That's sort of what I want," Katie admitted. "I want to lock myself in my room and put on the CD Doug gave me. It has this one song that gets me every time. I need to put away all my Michael souvenirs and have some time to cry out the rest of my tears in a less public place than Disneyland."

Christy thought about her next words and then decided to go ahead and say them. "Would you like me to stick around with you? I will if you want me to."

"No, you need to see Todd. You guys only have the weekends, and you were sick last weekend. Really, I'm fine. You go. Call me when you get back, okay?"

"Okay. And Katie?"

"Yeah?"

"I think you're doing great. You amaze me the way you put your mind to something and stick with it. I'm sure it would be a lot easier to get back together with Michael and let go of all the hurt. Instead, I see you willing to keep the hurt and let go of Michael. You're incredible. I love you, Katie."

Christy could hear Katie sniffling and felt bad for her.

"Thanks, Chris," Katie said in a wobbly voice. "I really needed to hear that. I love you, too. And I appreciate you more than you will ever know."

"Listen, Katie, if you want to talk any time this weekend, just call me at Bob and Marti's, okay? I mean it. Any hour of the day or night. You have the number, don't you?"

"Yes, I do. And thanks. I might do that. You have a fun

weekend, okay? Say hi to Todd for me. And if you see Doug, tell him I really appreciated the card he sent me last week. It cheered me up a lot."

"Okay, I will. Bye." Christy hung up and sat still for several minutes, thinking about Katie. She wished she could do something to make this Michael withdrawal easier. She thought about how every country-western song she had ever heard was true. Love hurts. Bad.

Friday after school, Christy hurried home to throw her stuff together for the weekend. Todd was coming to pick her up. She knew he would probably stay for dinner, but she wanted to be ready to leave whenever he was. She planned to discuss the prom during their ninety-minute drive to Bob and Marti's. If they did end up going, she would probably have a better choice of dresses at one of the big malls near her aunt and uncle's, and this would be the weekend to buy one.

Todd arrived a little past six o'clock, and Christy's mom had dinner all ready. Todd seemed like such a natural part of her family. Most of the dinner conversation flowed between Todd, Christy's little brother, and Christy's dad. As she cleared the table and served her mom's apple crisp for dessert, she realized there hadn't been even a pinch of a letup in the conversation. It was nice, really. Familiar. Secure.

For a brief instant, Christy wondered if life would be like this if she and Todd were married and invited her family over to their apartment for dinner. There was only one thing wrong with this picture. The apartment in her mind was the Swiss Family Robinson Tree House, and her parents and brother came by canoe. Even then, Christy couldn't quite picture herself wearing animal-skin garments with a bone in her hair, serving apple crisp in bowls carved out of gourds.

The jungle was Todd's dream, not necessarily hers. And that was a long, long way off. For now, there was a prom dress to worry about.

They didn't get on their way until after nine. As Christy crawled into the passenger seat of Gus, she felt more like stretching out in the back and taking a nap than initiating a lively conversation about the prom.

"Is it okay if I move these?" Christy asked Todd, holding up a handful of mail that was strewn on the passenger seat.

"Sure. Toss 'em on the floor."

"They might get lost," Christy said. "Are these letters supposed to be mailed?"

"No. It's my mail. I hadn't picked it up for almost a month, so there was a bunch."

They waved to Christy's mom and dad, who were standing on the front porch under the arched trellis covered with fragrant jasmine. Christy smiled with memories of the front porch and of Todd.

Todd cranked Gus into gear, and they puttered down Christy's quiet, tree-lined street and headed for the freeway. "You still feel up for going to the beach early tomorrow morning? You were looking a little tired after dinner."

"I am tired. I can't seem to get my energy back."

"Why don't you take a nap? I have a new tape from Doug. I'll put it on, and you can crash."

Christy knew Todd was right. She should sleep. They would be together lots more during the weekend. They would have time to talk about the prom later. Grabbing her jacket from off the back seat, she wadded it up into a pillow and leaned against the window.

Todd popped in the tape, and the mellow music came tiptoeing out, oblivious to the noisy rumble of the Volkswagen bus engine.

"This is nice," Christy said with her eyes closed. "Who is it?"

"It's a collection of different Christian artists. It's Doug's latest favorite."

"I wonder if this is the same CD he gave to Katie. She said she liked it and was going to lock herself in her room and listen to it all weekend." Then with a half smile she added, "I almost got a ticket when she took off her seat belt in the car and started rummaging through her pack, trying to find it on the way home from Bob and Marti's.

For the next hour or so, Christy dozed while Gus rumbled up the freeway. She didn't fully wake up until they arrived at Bob and Marti's.

"Kilikina," Todd said softly when he turned off the motor and it was suddenly quiet, "we're here."

"How are you doing?" Christy asked, stretching her stiff neck.

"I'm a little tired from driving, but I'm okay. You ready to go in?"

"Sure." Christy yawned and put on her jacket, ready to brace herself against the brisk chill off the ocean. She noticed something white on her lap. Holding it up to the light, she realized it was one of the letters tucked on the dashboard that had slipped off during the trip.

Todd came around and opened her door.

"Here," Christy said, handing him the letter. "It fell in my lap." She hopped out and zipped up the front of her jacket.

"Thanks," Todd said, taking the letter and placing it on the vacated passenger seat without even glancing at it.

Guys are weird, she thought. *No sense of curiosity. I'd never let my mail go for a month.*

"Let's walk on the beach," Christy said, feeling awake and alert, especially when the salty ocean scent hit her.

"Okay. We'd better tell Bob and Marti we're here, though," Todd suggested. He carried Christy's bag to the front door and knocked before turning the unlocked doorknob and walking in. "We're here!" he called out.

"Come on in," Bob answered. "I'm in the den."

Bob was pedaling away on his exercise bike, which was set up in front of the wide screen TV. "How was the ride up?" he asked, puffing for breath.

"I slept," Christy admitted.

"We're going for a walk on the beach," Todd said. "Just wanted to let you know we were here."

"Great! Beautiful night. Marti's in bed. I'll be turning in as soon as the news is over. How about if I leave the back door unlocked?"

"Thanks," Todd said. "See you tomorrow."

Todd reached for Christy's hand and led her out the back door and across the patio. They slipped off their shoes and dug their toes into the sand, running hand in hand down to the water.

Even though it was late, other people were out, riding bikes, walking along the beach, and hanging out on their patios, talking and laughing. Some partied with the music cranked up. None of this was unusual for a weekend in a beach community. The only thing a little out of the ordinary was the moon.

It was full, but not tinted the icy blue of winter and spring. Tonight it glowed with an amber hue. It hung right in the middle of the night sky, reflecting off the ocean. The face of the man in the moon appeared to be jovial, about to burst with some secret he hid behind his back.

Christy knew what the secret was. The tawny, golden promise of summer. She couldn't wait.

Todd and Christy stood close together, their feet burrowed in the cold sand at the edge of the foaming night waves. The water rushed up to tickle their ankles and then ran away before anyone could catch it in its game. Todd looped his thick arm around Christy's shoulders and rested his face against the top of her head.

"Oh, Kilikina," he whispered into her hair, "it feels so good to be with you, to hold you. You're in my thoughts day and night. I hold you in my heart."

This was not how Todd usually talked. Something deep inside Christy felt like weeping for joy. She had yearned to hear Todd say these things to her. She had waited a long time. And now it seemed as if she had only met him yesterday, and they would be together forever. She wanted to turn around, look him in the face, and say, "Todd, I love you."

But the memory of something Todd had said once stopped her. He had said he thought men should be the initiators, and women should be the responders. Christy knew that if the words "I love you" were ever to be spoken between them, they needed to come from Todd first.

She did her best to keep a guard on her heart. "I love being here with you," she said, nestling her head against his shoulder.

She felt like praying, the way Todd always did. In a rare, bold move, Christy spoke to her heavenly Father, sending her words into the night winds.

"Father, You made the heavens and the earth and all that is in them. You are such an awesome God! Thank You for making this perfect moon and this perfect night and for letting us be together." She was about to whisper her "Amen," when a strong, clear thought came to her. Without questioning it, she added, "And, Father, please prepare us both for what You have planned for our lives. We want to serve You and honor You in whatever You want us to do. Amen."

"Amen," Todd added, kissing Christy on the top of her head. "I'm going to get up early to go surfing tomorrow morning. You want to come with me?"

Christy couldn't believe Todd could switch gears so quickly. "Sure. When?"

"Around six. Will that give you enough sleep?"

Still startled by his abrupt switch, Christy said, "Six is fine. Where do you want me to meet you?"

"Out on Bob's patio." He released her from his hug and reached for her hand, slipping his fingers in between hers. "Ready to head back?"

"Okay," she said. She wasn't really. She could have stood wrapped up in Todd's arms for hours watching the moon, listening to the waves, feeling the cool water on her ankles, and dreaming with her eyes open.

They walked hand in hand back to Bob and Marti's patio, where Todd stopped and planted his feet in the sand. He turned Christy around so she faced him. Taking her face in both of his hands, he tilted her head up and looked into her eyes without saying a word. What did she read in his silver-blue eyes? Something powerful and intensely honest. Something stronger than she had ever seen before.

What did Todd read in her eyes? Did he see in her, as she had seen in the moon, a promise of summer, all warm and glowing with hope?

With a kiss as tender as rose petals across her lips, Todd said softly, "Meet me right here when the sun comes up."

"I'll be here," Christy promised. "Right here."

Todd let go. It seemed a hard thing for him to do.

Christy opened the back door and then locked it before quietly tiptoeing up the stairs to her prepared guest room. With a smile still on her freshly kissed lips, she set the alarm for 5:30 A.M.

CHAPTER TWELVE

Salt on Her Lips

The irritating buzzer seemed to be going off inside Christy's head. She turned over in bed and woke up fully, realizing the noise was coming from her alarm clock.

She squinted to see the time. "5:30? What was I thinking when I set this noisy thing for 5:30?" And then she remembered. With a clear purpose and distinct joy, Christy rolled out of bed and let her now-singing heart lead her reluctant, weary body into the shower.

The next time she checked the clock, it was 6:01 and she was ready. Quietly padding down the stairs, she left her prepared note on the entry table by the front door. Once before she had left for an early morning walk on the beach without telling anyone and had worried her aunt and uncle. That wouldn't happen this time.

Slipping out the back door and scanning the patio, her heart sank when she found no sign of Todd.

Maybe my clock is a little fast. Or maybe he's running behind. I know he wouldn't go out without me.

Christy made her way across the patio, her bare feet feeling the brunt of the concrete's cold. She walked to where she and Todd had stood last night and where he had said to meet him.

Christy searched for that exact spot. And there she stood, straight and tall, unmovable, eagerly scanning the horizon for a glimpse of Todd or his orange surfboard. She found neither.

Since Todd lived so close, she knew he would be walking. So she kept her eyes fixed to the left, the direction from which he would be coming. A few early risers were scattered here and there across the wide beach. It was a clear, chilly, glorious spring morning.

A guy with a white surfboard under his arm came riding by on a wide-tire beach bike. He did a double take when he noticed Christy standing there like a statue, so purposeful and yet, she suspected, so silly-looking.

She gave up the fantasy of waiting on the exact spot and took a seat at the patio table, facing the south and waiting.

Her feet were cold. She thought about going inside to put on some shoes and socks. Then when she came back, Todd might be standing there waiting for her. She hurried inside, grabbed her shoes and socks, slipped quietly downstairs, and went out the back door. Still no Todd. Now she was worried. The clock in her room had said 6:20.

Maybe I misunderstood. He must have said 6:30, and I thought he said 6:00. He'll be here any minute. Brrr! I'd love a cup of hot tea to warm up my hands.

Thinking she had ten more minutes, Christy went back inside, made herself and Todd some tea, and carried the mugs outside, one in each hand. Still no Todd. She sat down at the patio table and placed Todd's tea in front of the empty chair. Wrapping her fingers around her hot mug, she blew at the steam rising off the top and took a tiny sip. This experience was too painfully familiar. She had been through these kinds of ups and downs with Todd before.

After last night, Christy had felt certain she would never be left guessing where she stood with him again. She was in his heart. He had said so. He wouldn't forget and leave her. He couldn't.

Christy waited a few more minutes before taking the next sip. She looked down into the mug and saw a dark reflection of her doubt-filled eyes. There was something penetrating about seeing her own reflection. It was as if she was facing her own thoughts.

Let go.

The thought came to her as clearly as if it had been spoken aloud. Immediately she responded with a silent prayer.

You're right, Lord. I'm holding on to these fears and doubts when I should be holding on to You. I do let go now. I want to embrace Your truth.

She breathed in a fresh peace and looked up. Todd was standing there.

"Hi," he said. He looked awful.

"Are you okay?" Christy asked, putting down her mug and standing up.

"Yeah, sure, fine," Todd answered.

"Do you want some tea? I just made it. It's still hot."

"Thanks." Todd leaned his surfboard up against the lounge chair and sat down in the chair next to Christy. His wet suit made a slippery, rubber sound as he slid onto the vinyl chair pad. "I like tea," Todd said.

"Me too," Christy said, taking a sip and studying Todd's eyes. He hadn't looked directly at her yet.

"What is it?" Christy asked, leaning forward and placing her hand on top of Todd's. He responded by grasping her hand and entwining his fingers with hers. He squeezed her hand tightly. Almost too tightly. Then lifting her hand to his lips, he kissed her hand twice before placing it gently back on the table.

Forcing a smile, he looked at her and said, "Ask me again later, okay?" He took a sip of tea and looked into his mug, as if scrutinizing his reflection the way Christy had.

Ask you again later? When? In five minutes? In five months? What's wrong, Todd? I want to know now.

Christy remembered feeling this same way with Katie in the school parking lot when Katie wouldn't tell her what was wrong. Todd had advised Christy to wait until Katie was ready to talk. He said the test of true love was found not in our trying to hold our friends tighter but in the strength to let them go. Christy would now, with great determination, apply Todd's advice to his own situation. She couldn't begin to imagine what was wrong.

They walked down to the water with their arms around each other. She had never felt him hold on to her this closely before. They stopped at the crest in the dry sand, right before it turned wet from the persistent morning tide.

Todd scanned the water and then let go of Christy. He reached for the leash at the end of his board and pulled apart the Velcro strap. It sounded like fabric ripping. Todd fastened the leash to his ankle and zipped his wet suit up to his chin. Then marching down to the water, he walked right into the first wave, ducking under and getting himself soaked before bobbing up, shaking the wet from his hair, and mounting his surfboard. He paddled out to a cluster of about a dozen other surfers and took his place sitting on his board with his legs dangling in the water.

This is hard, Christy thought. *How long will I have to wait before he tells me what's bothering him? I thought I had Todd all figured out, and now this morning, I feel as if I don't even know him.*

For the next half hour, Christy watched, prayed, and waited. Todd caught maybe three waves during that whole time. There weren't very many big ones, and Christy knew enough about surfer etiquette to know that Todd would never cut off another guy if he took the wave first. She felt relieved and a tiny bit nervous when she realized he had caught a wave and was riding it all the way to shore.

Todd emerged from the water, scooped his board under his arm, and jogged up to where Christy sat. When he was still several yards away, he stopped, tilted his head back, and shook his sun-bleached hair. She had watched him shake out his hair like that a dozen times. Watching him now, it made Todd seem familiar once again.

"I made a decision," Todd said, planting his board upright in the sand and sitting down next to Christy in the sand. He reached over and took her hand. She responded by slipping her small hand into his cold one and giving it a squeeze. Todd's thumb rested on Christy's gold ID bracelet, and she could feel him instinctively rub his thumb back and forth over the word "Forever" engraved on the bracelet.

With his gaze fixed out on the ocean, Todd squinted his eyes against the brilliant blue. Turning back to face Christy, he looked directly at her. Now the brilliant blue was in his eyes.

"Kilikina, I made a decision." He paused. "You know that letter you showed me last night in the van? I opened it when I got home. It was from a mission organization. You see, I wrote to them last summer and sent in an application for a short-term mission assignment. Three to four years. They wrote back to tell me I was accepted. They want me there in two weeks."

For Christy, it was as if the whole world had just stopped. She couldn't hear the waves or feel the ocean breeze on her face. All she heard were Todd's words frozen in the air between them. She couldn't think or feel or breathe.

"I was pretty amazed," Todd went on. "Everything appears to be set up and ready for me to walk right into the position after the training. It's what I've always wanted to do."

Christy could feel the numbing effect of Todd's words begin to thaw. As it did, she felt as if a thousand needles were piercing her heart.

Todd took a deep breath. He let go of Christy's hand and turned to face her more squarely. He leaned closer and said, "I prayed all night. I didn't sleep at all. When I thought about leaving you, it tore me up inside. When I thought about staying, I had peace. That's how I knew what my decision was. I'm going to call them on Monday and tell them I can't take the position."

"You're going to what?" Christy couldn't believe she had heard correctly.

"I'm turning it down. I can't go now. Not with us being so close. A year ago I could have gone. Six months ago, maybe. But not now. It's like I told you at Disneyland, I've never had anybody. Now I have you. I don't take that lightly. You are God's gift to me, Kilikina. I can't leave you. Not now. Not ever."

Christy closed her eyes and caught her breath. Her heart was pounding wildly. This whole conversation seemed like a bizarre dream. She tried to take in all that Todd had said. She felt relieved that he had made his decision based on what would be best for them. She couldn't bear the thought of being separated from him any more than he apparently could stand the idea of being away from her. But did he mean it deep down inside?

"Todd, are you absolutely sure? You've always wanted to be a missionary."

"And I always wanted," Todd paused, searching for the right words, "well, I've always wanted other things, too."

"Todd, are you sure you want to give up this opportunity?" Christy asked, looking him in the eye.

"Yes, I'm sure."

"And you're giving it up because of me or because of us?"

A smile crept onto Todd's face, causing his dimple to appear on his right cheek. Christy had never seen him look so vulnerable. "Yes, because of you, because of us. You mean more to me than anything, Kilikina." Then he leaned over and kissed her.

When he drew away, Christy could taste the salt on her lips. She had tasted the salt of her own tears before, but she wasn't prepared for the taste of ocean water in his kiss. It seemed different than any of Todd's other kisses. This had a bit of a sting to it.

"Come on," Todd said, standing up and offering Christy his hand. "Let's get some breakfast. We have the whole day to spend together. What would you like to do?"

Christy rose to her feet and brushed the sand off her backside. "I don't know. Give me a minute here. This whole thing has hit me by surprise. First, I imagined all the possible things that could be bothering you, then you tell me you've been offered a position with a mission for three to four years, and then you say you're not going. It's a bit much for me to digest in one bite."

"You're right," Todd said. "I had all night to think it over. I feel so relieved that I told you. I wasn't going to. I was going to act as if I'd never received the letter. I'm glad I told you."

Christy couldn't exactly say the same.

When they reached Bob and Marti's, Todd hosed off his board and his wet suit and left them to dry on the patio.

"Do you think Bob would mind if I borrowed a pair of shorts and a T-shirt?" Todd indicated the stack of freshly laundered clothes lying on the dryer in the laundry room.

"I'm sure it would be fine; you know how easygoing Uncle Bob is."

Helping himself to a pair of khaki shorts and a white T-shirt,

Todd went into the downstairs bathroom to shower and change.

Apparently Bob and Marti weren't up yet. The house was still quiet. Christy noticed it was almost eight o'clock.

Todd emerged from the bathroom and joined Christy in the kitchen. "Do you want to eat here or go out?"

"Let's stay here," Christy suggested. "Does cereal sound okay?" She pulled two boxes from the cupboard.

"Sure." Todd opened the refrigerator and pulled out a gallon of milk. "Is it okay if we eat by the TV?"

"I guess," Christy said.

"Didn't you grow up watching Saturday morning cartoons while you ate your cereal?"

"No, we weren't allowed to eat in the living room."

"Must be one of the advantages of being an only child raised by one parent who was never home. There weren't too many things I wasn't allowed to do."

Christy and Todd carefully carried their cereal bowls into the den and switched on the TV with the volume low so they wouldn't wake anyone up. Christy finished eating first and placed her empty bowl on the floor. Then she grabbed one of her grandmother's crocheted blankets out of the basket by the wall and stretched out on the plush love seat. She curled up with a pillow under her head. With heavy eyelids and a heart full of emotions, Christy tried to pay attention to the cartoon while listening to Todd's rhythmic crunch of cereal. Before long, Todd's crunching ceased, and Christy gave in to the sleep dust that had collected on her eyelids. She couldn't possibly keep her eyes open when her lids weighed so much.

Aunt Marti's voice woke Christy some time later. Christy lifted her still-groggy head and looked around for Marti's location. She was standing directly behind the love seat. "How long have you two been sleeping here?" Marti wanted to know.

"I don't know," Christy mumbled. She noticed Todd was asleep, too, stretched out on the couch. He had slept through Marti's entrance.

"Shh," Christy said, pressing her finger to her lips. "He didn't get much sleep last night."

"And why was that?"

"It's a long story," Christy said.

"Could it be because he never went home last night?"

"Aunt Marti!" Christy said sharply. "He didn't stay here all night. We both got up early because Todd went surfing while I watched him. We came in a little while ago, and I guess we were both super-tired."

"Oh," Marti said with a twittering laugh. "Then by all means, don't let me bother you. I'll turn off the TV so you can get some more sleep."

The minute the sound went off, Todd opened his eyes and said, "What's going on?"

Christy thought it was funny. She had seen her dad respond the same way. As long as the TV was on, he could snore away, sound asleep in his recliner. The minute the TV was turned off, he would wake up.

"Go back to sleep," Marti said. "Would you like a blanket?"

"No, I'm fine," Todd said, sitting up and running his fingers through the sides of his hair. "Man, I really conked out."

"It's only 10:30," Marti said. "Why don't you sleep some more? It's Saturday, you know."

"We must have slept for two hours! Did you sleep too, Christy?"

"I think I fell asleep before you did," she said, yawning and sticking her bare feet out from under the crocheted blanket.

"Well, as long as you're both up, would you like to join Robert and me for a leisurely brunch?"

Twenty-five minutes later, Christy and Todd were following Bob and Marti through the buffet line at a nearby resort hotel and loading their plates with a variety of fancy foods. To be specific, Todd was loading his plate. Christy was picking and choosing carefully. She didn't feel hungry. Instead, she felt more like she had an upset stomach. When she sat down to eat, she realized her queasy stomach was because of Todd's letter and his turning down the opportunity.

Christy lifted her fork to her mouth and bit into a ripe strawberry. Swallowing the small bite, she licked her lips. They tasted salty.

She took another bite of the strawberry, fully expecting it to taste sweet this time. Again, it tasted salty. Was it the strawberry? Or was it the acid from her grumbling stomach tainting the strawberry?

Todd's news had been unsettling. But when Christy considered the alternative, his decision was good news. She should be happy. Relieved. Delighted.

She tried to silently pray and ask God to give her His peace the way Todd said he had peace. Even though Todd seemed settled with his decision, she wondered if one day he might resent her for holding him back from his dream. On the other hand, would Christy end up resenting God if someday He took Todd away?

CHAPTER THIRTEEN

Let Go

"Bob said he would go with me to the men's prayer breakfast on Tuesday morning," Todd said enthusiastically. "Did I tell you that?"

Their weekend together had flown by, and Todd and Christy were now chugging down the freeway on their way to Christy's house.

"I think my aunt enjoyed church this morning a little more than she did a couple weeks ago. At least she wasn't as critical. Uncle Bob said he liked it," Christy said. Her voice quavered as they went over a rough spot on the freeway. Gus passed every bump along to his passengers. "You have a great church. I think they would be comfortable there, if they decided to be involved."

"Hopefully not too comfortable," Todd said. "We want them to squirm when the reality of heaven and hell is presented. They need to get saved, not just churched."

Christy agreed. They drove on down the freeway, each enveloped in private thoughts. It had been a difficult weekend for Christy ever since Todd had made his announcement on the beach. Todd seemed normal, relaxed, and content. Christy hadn't yet found the peace he had.

Last night her sleep had been sparse. What little sleep she did get was punctuated by fitful dreams. The worst was a nightmare she had had once before, and in that same room.

It was during the summer of the year she gave her heart to the Lord, just before she had made that big decision. She had dreamed she was in the ocean and seaweed had become tangled around her legs and in her hair, pulling her farther and farther down to the bottom of the ocean. That's when the dream had ended the first time she had dreamed it.

But last night it had kept going. She had struggled against the seaweed, pulling and kicking. But she rapidly ran out of air. Then she had heard a voice say, "Let go." She relaxed, and immediately she was released, and her body had floated to the surface, where she drew in the sweet, fresh air.

Christy didn't know what it meant.

Maybe what's bothering me is that we haven't talked about the prom. I have to know by tomorrow, since the prom is only two weeks away. Once we decide, I'll feel more settled and secure.

Christy tried to think of how to bring up the subject. She could talk to Todd about anything. Why did she feel so tongue-tied about this?

Todd talked a little about school ending next week for him, and how he needed to find a summer job. "I might even take a class or two in summer school, since I'm not going anywhere."

Christy thought she detected a hint of sadness or disappointment in his voice. But then, summer school never sounded interesting to Christy.

Anxious to keep the plans for their future together headed in a positive direction, Christy said, "I feel relieved about finally deciding to go to Palomar in the fall. I'll still be at home, which will save money. I'll still work at the pet store, and we'll have lots of time to spend together. I think Katie's going to Palomar, too."

"Cool," Todd said calmly. "It's going to be great being together this summer, isn't it? Long, sunny days on the beach."

Suddenly Todd turned off the freeway. "I have an idea. Let's
go down to the beach and watch the sunset. If we hurry, we can
make it."

He turned right and then left and then left again as if he knew
where he was going. Todd had told Christy before that there was
a favorite spot for surfers somewhere along here.

They pulled into San Clemente State Beach and stopped at
the small booth where a uniformed park ranger checked cars in
and out. Fees were posted on the window for day use, camping,
etc.

"How much will it cost for us to go down and watch the sunset?" Todd asked.

The ranger pushed up his wire-rimmed glasses and glanced at
Todd, then smiled at Christy. "For you two, how about free?"

"Cool," Todd said.

"Here, let me give you a half-hour pass. Stick it on your window."

"Thanks," Todd said, and he gave the ranger a Hawaiian
surfer "hang loose" gesture. The ranger returned the universal
sign, and Gus puttered into the campground.

"This is a great place to go camping," Todd observed. "We
should get a bunch of us together this summer and rent a spot for
a week."

"Sounds like fun," Christy said.

"We could have a huge campout the last week of summer. Surf
all day. Sing around the campfire at night. Wouldn't that be great!
We could call it Summer Fall Out."

Christy had to smile at Todd's enthusiasm. He was definitely a visionary. Yet she wondered if he wasn't trying a little too hard to speak their future into being, to plan his own adventures to take the place of the ones he would have had in Papua New Guinea.

They parked in the day-use lot, and Todd led Christy down a wide but steep dirt trail to the beach.

"It's a long way down there," Christy said. "Is this the only trail?"

"This is the main path," Todd said. "It's the safest way to go."

They passed several people who were walking up, burdened with armloads of beach gear. They all seemed to be huffing and puffing from the climb.

That's going to be us going back! Good thing we're not carrying beach chairs and surfboards.

Todd continued to hold Christy's hand when they reached the bottom of the trail. They climbed over a railroad track and down a sand dune before they were actually on the beach.

The sight that greeted them was worth the hike. Mr. Sun was just beginning to dip his sizzling toes into the cool, blue ocean. The sky all around the sun looked like a huge, pastel beach towel lovingly wrapped around him to brace him from the chill of the water.

"It's beautiful," Christy whispered.

Todd wrapped his arm around her. They stood together in silent awe, watching the sunset. All Christy could think of was how this was what she had always wanted, to be held in Todd's arms as well as in his heart.

Just as the last golden drop of sun melted into the ocean, Christy closed her eyes and drew in a deep draught of the sea air.

"Did you know," Todd said softly, "that the setting sun looks so huge from the island of Papua New Guinea that it almost looks as if you're on another planet? I've seen pictures."

Then, as had happened with her reflection in her cup of tea and in her disturbing dream, Christy heard those two piercing words, "Let go."

She knew what she had to do. Turning to face Todd, she said, "Pictures aren't enough for you, Todd. You have to go."

"I will. Someday. Lord willing," he said casually.

"Don't you see, Todd? The Lord is willing. This is your 'some-day.' Your opportunity to go on the mission field is now. You have to go."

Their eyes locked in silent communion.

"God has been telling me something, Todd. He's been telling me to let you go. I don't want to, but I need to obey Him."

Todd paused and said, "Maybe I should tell them I can only go for the summer. That way I'll only be gone a few months. A few weeks, really. We'll be back together in the fall."

Christy shook her head. "It can't be like that, Todd. You have to go for as long as God tells you to go. And as long as I've known you, God has been telling you to go. His mark is on your life, Todd. It's obvious. You need to obey him."

"Kilikina," Todd said, grasping Christy by the shoulders, "do you realize what you're saying? If I go, I may never come back."

"I know." Christy's reply was barely a whisper. She reached for the bracelet on her right wrist and released the lock. Then taking Todd's hand, she placed the "Forever" bracelet in his palm and closed his fingers around it.

"Todd," she whispered, forcing the words out, "the Lord bless you and keep you. The Lord make His face to shine upon you and give you His peace. And may you always love Jesus more than anything else. Even more than me."

Todd crumbled to the sand like a man who had been run

through with a sword. Burying his face in his hands, he wept.

Christy stood on wobbly legs. *What have I done? Oh, Father God, why do I have to let him go?*

Slowly lowering her quivering body to the sand beside Todd, Christy cried until all she could taste was the salty tears on her lips.

They drove the rest of the way home in silence. A thick mantle hung over them, entwining them even in their separation. To Christy it seemed like a bad dream. Someone else had let go of Todd. Not her! He wasn't really going to go.

They pulled into Christy's driveway, and Todd turned off the motor. Without saying anything, he got out of Gus and came around to Christy's side to open the door for her. She stepped down and waited while he grabbed her luggage from the backseat. They walked to the front door.

Todd stopped her under the trellis of wildly fragrant white jasmine. With tears in his eyes, he said in a hoarse voice, "I'm keeping this." He lifted his hand to reveal the "Forever" bracelet looped between his fingers. "If God ever brings us together again in this world, I'm putting this back on your wrist, and that time, my Kilikina, it will stay on forever."

He stared at her through blurry eyes for a long minute, and then without a hug, a kiss, or even a good-bye, Todd turned to go. He walked away and never looked back.

The next day Christy stayed home from school. Her mom understood and let her have the day to cry alone. That's all she did. The more she cried, the more she hurt and the more utterly exhausted she felt.

At about four o'clock there was a gentle tap on her bedroom door. "Hi," Katie said, poking her head inside. "I heard. Doug called me this morning."

She sat down on the side of Christy's bed and with extra tenderness said, "I'm sorry, Christy."

"I can't believe I did it, Katie. Why did I? I keep going over the whole thing in my mind, and I think I must be crazy."

"Weird," Katie corrected her. "Remember? God is weird. We are tweaked. Whenever you do something weird, you're becoming a little more godly. And believe me, what you did was weird!"

Christy reached for a tissue and dabbed her swollen eyes.

"Doug said Todd told him last night that you loved him enough to let him go and that you motivated him to obey God's call when he was ready to forget it. That's incredible, Christy. That's like that verse about there being no greater love than to lay down your life for your friend. I don't know how you did it. I couldn't have."

"What do you mean? You did. You're the one who broke up with Michael, remember?"

"That was different."

"I don't know, Katie. A broken heart is a broken heart."

"If I hurt so much over Michael, I can't imagine how much you must be hurting over Todd. What can I do?"

"Nothing. Tell me I did the right thing."

Katie let out a laugh. "How can you have any doubts? Of course you did the right thing! You gave nobility a face, Christy."

"Nobility a what?" Christy propped herself up on her arm and scrutinized Katie's expression.

Katie smiled. "Can I just say, yes, Christina Juliet Miller, you did the right thing. You gave God a gift: Todd, free and clear. And there's one thing I know for sure. You can never out-give God. I can't wait to see what God is going to give you!"

"I wish I could have your optimism, Katie."

"You will. It just takes a little time. What's that bit of wisdom you told me several weeks ago? Oh, yes. The feelings don't come in the same envelope. They'll catch up. Until then, here's Doug's CD. It'll help. My favorite song is number seven. It's a good song to cry along with."

"Thanks. You know, Katie, I keep thinking what I had with Todd wasn't real. It was too perfect. He was too perfect. It was a sort of dream and now it's time for me to wake up and grow up. I'm a different person now at seventeen than I was when I met him. But I'm still too young to be as serious as I was becoming with him. This is all probably for the best."

"Keep telling yourself stuff like that," Katie said with a knowing smile. "The only part I'll agree with for now is that with God, things do tend to turn out for the best. Think you'll be back in school tomorrow?"

"Yes, I have a final in Spanish. Thanks for coming over."

Katie gave Christy a hug and said, "That's what best friends are for. Now listen, I'm going to pick you up for school tomorrow morning. Wear something you really like so you'll feel good about yourself. I'll bring an extra Twinkie for you for lunch."

Katie kept her word, and at lunch she presented Christy with a Twinkie.

"I thought you were done with Twinkies," Christy said.

"Not completely. I have to admit I'm still trying to find a balance between Twinkies and Tofu."

Christy laughed.

"Did I tell you that Fred was at church again yesterday?" Katie asked. "He bought himself a Bible, and I saw him carrying it to school today. Isn't that incredible? Who would have ever guessed?"

"Katie," Christy asked cautiously, "are you really, truly over

Michael? You seem to be doing so well, but are the feelings really gone?''

Katie turned solemn. "Maybe I'm still working on a balance there, too. I don't think the feelings will ever be gone completely. It's still hard when I see him, even though I know I did the right thing. Remember when we talked about being in love? I think what we decided is true. You can be in love with someone and yet never marry him. A little part of that person will always be hidden somewhere in a secret garden deep inside your heart.''

As Katie spoke, the tears welled up in Christy's eyes. It still hurt so much.

"The thing is, Christy, I never compromised my standards or morals with Michael, and so in that area, I have no regrets. You should never have any regrets with Todd, either. You loved him. Face it, you always will. Now go on with your life. God is near to the brokenhearted, and it just so happens that you and I both qualify for that position.''

Between her tears and her Twinkie, Christy forced a smile.

"And," Katie added, holding her head high, "I just so happen to think that being near to God is a wonderfully safe place to be.''

Christy thought of Katie's words often as she went through the motions of life that week. Nights were the hardest. She lay awake for long hours in the darkness, exhausting her imagination as she hoped her circumstances would change and fighting off the unanswerable questions. Whenever the phone rang, her heart froze. Each day she checked the mail. But Todd had never written to her before. He wouldn't now. And he wouldn't call, either. He was gone for good.

CHAPTER FOURTEEN

The Secret Revealed

Christy made it through the weekend with Katie's help and even went to church on Sunday. Fred sat with them during the service. Afterward they walked out to the church parking lot together, and Fred followed Christy to her car.

Right in front of her parents and her brother, he said, "Christy, as you know, the senior prom is this Friday. I would be honored if you would go with me."

Christy had to give the guy credit for perseverance. "Thanks for asking me, Fred. I really mean that. I just can't go. Not with you. Not with anyone. You need to find someone fun to go with and have a great time. You deserve it."

Fred hung his head and said, "I guess I can take a hint." With that, he left.

A short time after they had reached home, Katie called. "Go ahead. Guess," she said.

"Guess what?"

"Guess what I'm doing this Friday?"

"I give up."

"I'm going to the prom. With Fred."

There was complete silence.

"Well?" Katie prodded.

Christy burst out laughing. It was the first time in more than a week that she had laughed, and it felt good.

"I think it's great. You'll have so much fun!"

"At least he's a Christian," Katie said. "That's a step in the right direction for me."

"He'll treat you like a queen," Christy predicted. "I'm glad you're going with him. Fred deserves the best, and that's what you are."

It wasn't until that night that Christy felt the impact of Katie's call. As long as they were both staying home from the prom, it felt okay. The two of them could rent old movies and commiserate. Now Katie had a date, and it was a date with someone who had initially asked Christy.

On Thursday night a phone call came for Christy. It was Doug.

"How are you doing?" he asked tenderly.

"Sometimes okay, other times not so okay," she answered.

"Would you be willing to do me a favor?" Doug asked. "Would you let me take you out to dinner tomorrow night? You see, I'm at the airport right now, and Todd just left. I feel as if I lost my best friend, and I was wondering if you could cheer me up."

Something inside Christy froze all over again at the news that Todd was gone. All her fantasies of Todd not really leaving disappeared. She felt the bitter sting of reality.

"You would have to wear something nice," Doug was saying. "The restaurant I'd like to go to is kind of fancy. So how about it? Could you do me this one favor?"

"All right," Christy said. That was about the extent of the words she could find.

"Awesome," Doug said. "I'll pick you up at 6:30, okay?"

"Okay. Bye."

Christy crawled into bed, still feeling numb, and cried herself to sleep.

The next morning she woke up feeling almost relieved. As long as Todd was still in California, she had held on to some thin strands of hope that something would change. Now he was gone. Tonight was the prom, and although she wasn't going, she would be dressing up and having dinner with Doug at a nice restaurant. That wasn't such a bad thing.

She left school at noon and went to Katie's house to help her dress for the prom. Katie seemed so excited. But after Christy finished applying Katie's makeup, Katie turned somber.

"You know," she said, examining her image in the mirror, "I've been wondering if Michael will be there tonight. I really wish I was going with him instead of Fred. I did spend nearly all of my senior year with him."

Christy cast an understanding smile at Katie's pretty reflection. "I know exactly what you're feeling."

"You wish you were going out with Todd tonight instead of Mr. Counselor-to-All-Brokenhearted-Women, don't you?"

"Well, yes, but . . ."

"But you have to take what you can get, right?" Katie said.

"Something like that."

Katie turned and faced Christy, examining her through narrowed green eyes. Christy knew Katie was looking for something that couldn't be found on the surface. "Do you think Todd is going to come back? Or do you think he's really gone for good?"

Christy couldn't turn from her friend's intense gaze, so she met it head-on and let Katie see the tears in her eyes. "Yes," Christy said, "I think he's really gone. For good."

Tears welled up in Katie's eyes as she said, "I'm so sorry, Christy."

Forcing a smile, Christy said, "Don't you dare start to cry, Katie! You'll ruin the perfect job I did on your makeup."

Her expression still serious, Katie said, "You did the right thing, Christy. God will have someone else for you. I know I didn't want to hear that right after Michael, but I believe it now. For both of us. God has a couple of peculiar treasures, like that Bible verse says, for us. What do you think?"

A giggle bubbled up inside of Christy, and she said, "I think if you're looking for peculiar, look no farther! Fred definitely qualifies."

Katie laughed and said in a game-show-host voice, "The qualifications are 'peculiar' and 'treasure.' Contestants who only fall into one category and not both are automatically disqualified."

Christy laughed and said, "And maybe Fred does qualify."

She was still smiling ten minutes later when she left Katie's to hurry home and begin her own beautification ritual. She had to admit, it was kind of exciting and mysterious to think of who her peculiar treasure might be if it wasn't Todd.

Humming to herself, Christy showered and washed, dried, and curled her hair. When she combed it out, she started playing with it, trying to come up with a new hair-style. Something fun and different. She needed a fresh start. She ended up taking two small portions of her hair from right behind each ear and braiding them. Then taking the two braids and crisscrossing them over the top of her head and securing the ends with hidden bobby pins, she created a hair headband. It looked kind of cute, she decided.

Choosing a dress was easy. Aunt Marti had bought one for her before Christmas, assuming she would have lots of Christmas parties and dances to go to. In the end, Christy had only worn it on Christmas Eve when her family went to the candlelight service at church. It was black velvet, and she liked the way it fit.

Doug arrived right at 6:30, wearing a striking black suit. He handed her a corsage and said, "If you don't want to wear it, that's okay. You can just hold it if you want. It smells nice."

Christy lifted the white gardenia from the plastic box and sniffed its rich, sweet fragrance.

"I do want to wear it," Christy said. "Right here so I can smell it all night."

Doug pinned on the corsage, and with his little-boy grin lighting up his face, he said, "You look absolutely gorgeous. Did you know that?"

Christy felt herself blush, mostly because her parents were standing close enough to hear Doug's compliment.

She felt a little awkward when her mom wanted to take pictures, and Christy wasn't sure what to do with her hands. She ended up clutching her beaded purse in front of her with her hands crossed at the wrists. Doug stood next to her but didn't touch her. It all felt a little strange, a little like going out on a first date.

But it was a nice awkwardness. Much nicer than staying at home alone on prom night.

Doug helped Christy up into the cab of his yellow Toyota truck and apologized for not renting a limo. Christy laughed and said she felt more at home in his truck anyway.

All the way to the restaurant in San Diego, Doug and Christy reminisced about the things they had done together over the past three years. Doug was with Todd the day Christy met him on the beach at Newport. A wild wave had seized her gangly fourteen-year-old frame and had tumbled her ashore, draped with seaweed, right at Doug and Todd's feet. It was Doug's body board she had then used to master the waves that had dumped her onto the beach.

"I'll never forget the night we had a campfire on the beach," Doug said. "We were all going around the circle praying, and you were sitting next to me. In your prayer you thanked God for coming into your life. That was the first any of us knew you had become a Christian."

"That was the first time I ever had the wind nearly knocked out of me by one of your hugs!" Christy said. "Oh, and remember the time you came over to my aunt and uncle's, and when I answered the door with that basketful of laundry, I tripped and you and I both ended up in a tumble with all my dirty clothes?"

Doug laughed. "Do you remember when you and Katie came down to San Diego, and we were doing the dishes at Stephanie's apartment? We were throwing something up on the ceiling."

"It was that little Mr. Gizmo you got out of the cereal box," Christy said.

"All I remember is it dropped off the ceiling into your hair."

"That was a fun time," Christy agreed. "And remember the houseboat trip when you went jet skiing with that girl, Natalie? And then a couple of weeks later Katie and Michael tried to set you up at the pet store. Michael said he had come to defend his sister's honor, and his sister was supposedly Natalie?"

Doug nodded as he drove into the Mission Bay area of San Diego. "But that wasn't such a great memory. I accidentally knocked you nearly unconscious."

"It wasn't your fault," Christy said. "It's funny now."

She realized they had been talking and laughing the whole way. She felt unexpectedly lighthearted.

"What about that time," Doug continued, "when we all went ice skating, and you skated with me to make Todd jealous, and

Todd ended up skating with those two junior high girls?"

"Wait a minute. You knew I was trying to make Todd jealous?"

"Christy," Doug said, shooting her a knowing glance, "yeah. And did you know I was trying to make Todd jealous that time I buried my nose in your hair to smell your green apple perm, right when Todd drove by?"

Christy was shocked. "You did that on purpose?"

"Not at first. I really was only going to sniff your hair. Then when I heard ol' Gus chugging down the street, I decided to linger a little longer."

"You beast!" Christy said, playfully swatting Doug with her purse.

"Oh, that's nothing," Doug said. "My favorite was being your valet when Rick took you to the Villa Nova. I loved the look on his face when I gave you a hug."

"I forgot about that night," Christy said. "Did you know that Rick actually stole the bracelet Todd gave me and hocked it at a jeweler's? Did he ever tell you that when you were roommates last year? I paid every week to get it back. Well, that is until some mystery guy went into the jeweler's and paid more than a hundred bucks for me to get it back."

"Yeah, I knew that," Doug said, his voice quieting down.

Christy's heart stopped. For some reason Doug's response made her blurt out, "It was you."

Doug looked straight ahead and kept driving.

"All the jeweler would tell me was it was some guy. And it was you, wasn't it, Doug?"

"Yep. It was me. You weren't ever supposed to find out."

"Why?" Christy asked, still overwhelmed at Doug's kindness, not only with the bracelet but also in all the other situations they had been reminiscing about. And he had been so sweet and understanding with Katie at Disneyland. Not to mention being so nice to her tonight.

Doug pulled off the freeway and stopped at a red light. "Christy, do you remember when we went to the Rose Parade, and you asked if I was just being nice to you because Todd asked me to keep an eye on you?"

She sort of remembered. Doug seemed to be studying her expression before giving her his explanation.

"I guess," she said.

Doug looked away and let out a deep breath. "Well," he said, his cheerful disposition blowing away the momentary dark clouds, "let's just say I knew how much that bracelet meant to you."

"Thanks, Doug" was all Christy could find to say as he pulled into the parking lot of a gorgeous restaurant that looked like an old clipper ship. "I appreciate you being here for me, especially tonight. You're a very special friend."

"A very special friend," Doug muttered. "Just friends."

"What?" Christy asked, not sure she had heard what he said.

Doug turned off the engine. "Nothing," he said. "Enough of the serious stuff. Let's have some fun."

Doug came around and opened the door. Taking Christy's hand, he helped her down from the truck. "Think of tonight as your very own private prom night with your special friend. And enjoy every minute of it, okay?"

"I will, Doug. I will."

As Doug and Christy walked arm in arm into the restaurant, a smile tiptoed onto Christy's lips. She felt a peculiar happiness, but she wasn't sure why. All she knew was that deep inside, the forever part of her heart was still very much alive.

Don't Miss These Captivating Stories in
THE CHRISTY MILLER SERIES

THE SIERRA JENSEN SERIES

If you've enjoyed reading about Christy Miller,
you'll love reading about Christy's friend Sierra Jensen.

#1 • Only You, Sierra
When her family moves to another state, Sierra dreads going to a new high school—until she meets Paul.

#2 • In Your Dreams
Just when events in Sierra's life start to look up—she even gets asked out on a date—Sierra runs into Paul.

#3 • Don't You Wish
Sierra is excited about visiting Christy Miller in California during Easter break. Unfortunately, her sister, Tawni, decides to go with her.

#4 • Close Your Eyes
Sierra experiences a sticky situation when Paul comes over for dinner and Randy shows up at the same time.

#5 • Without A Doubt
When handsome Drake reveals his interest in Sierra, life gets complicated.

#6 • With This Ring
Sierra couldn't be happier when she goes to Southern California to join Christy Miller and their friends for Doug and Tracy's wedding.

#7 • Open Your Heart
When Sierra's friend Christy Miller receives a scholarship from a university in Switzerland, she invites Sierra to go with her and Aunt Marti to visit the school.

#8 • Time Will Tell
After an exciting summer in Southern California and Switzerland, Sierra returns home to several unsettled relationships.

#9 • Now Picture This
When Sierra and Paul start corresponding, she imagines him as her boyfriend and soon begins neglecting her family and friends.

#10 • Hold On Tight
Sierra joins her brother and several friends on a road trip to Southern California to visit potential colleges.

#11 • Closer Than Ever
When Paul doesn't show up for her graduation party and news comes that a flight from London has crashed, Sierra frantically worries about the future.

#12 • Take My Hand
A costly misunderstanding leaves Sierra anxious as she says goodbye to Portland and heads off to California for her freshman year of college.

FOCUS ON THE FAMILY®
LIKE THIS BOOK?

Then you'll love *Brio* magazine! Written especially for teen girls, it's packed each month with 32 pages on everything from fiction and faith to fashion, food . . . even guys! Best of all, it's all from a Christian perspective! But don't just take our word for it. Instead, see for yourself by requesting a complimentary copy.

Simply write Focus on the Family, Colorado Springs, CO 80995 (in Canada, write P.O. Box 9800, Stn. Terminal, Vancouver, B.C. V6B 4G3) and mention that you saw this offer in the back of this book. You may also call 1-800-232-6459 (in Canada, call 1-800-661-9800).

You may also visit our Web site (www.family.org) to learn more about the ministry or find out if there is a Focus on the Family office in your country.

Want to become everyone's favorite baby-sitter? Then *The Ultimate Baby-Sitter's Survival Guide* is for you! It's packed with page after page of practical information and ways to stay in control; organize mealtime, bath time and bedtime; and handle emergency situations. It also features an entire section of safe, creative and downright crazy indoor and outdoor activities that will keep kids challenged, entertained and away from the television. Easy-to-read and reference, it's the ideal book for providing the best care to children, earning money and having fun at the same time.

Call Focus on the Family at the number above, or check out your local Christian bookstore.

Focus on the Family is an organization that is dedicated to helping you and your family establish lasting, loving relationships with each other and the Lord. It's why we exist! If we can assist you or your family in any way, please feel free to contact us. We'd love to hear from you!